MO FANNING

THIS IS (NOT) AMERICA

A collection of short stories

First published by Spring Street Books 2020

Copyright © 2020 by Mo Fanning

Second edition

All rights reserved. No part of this publication may be reproduced, stored or transmitted in any form or by any means, electronic, mechanical, photocopying, recording, scanning, or otherwise without written permission from the publisher. It is illegal to copy this book, post it to a website, or distribute it by any other means without permission.

This novel is entirely a work of fiction. The names, characters and incidents portrayed in it are the work of the author's imagination. Any resemblance to actual persons, living or dead, events or localities is entirely coincidental.

Mo Fanning asserts the moral right to be identified as the author of this work.

ISBN: 978-0-9935571-2-5

Spring Street Books
Stourbridge, Great Britain

mofanning.co.uk

For Mark, as always

I always try to balance the light with the heavy - a few tears of human spirit in with the sequins and the fringes.

Bette Middler

Acknowledgement

I published my first anthology of short stories in 2012. 'Shorts' was a rushed affair, curated at a time of personal turmoil. It was a project intended to prove to myself I still had the will to be creative. Given I didn't write another word for two years, things didn't really work out. In 2018, I revisited the stories and was struck by how dark my writing had become. I added new tales and reworked existing ones.

This revised anthology still comes with a high body count, but I sincerely hope that the overall message has changed to one of hope. Life is very short and whilst there are people deserving of the effort it takes to hate, there are many more worth knowing.

Which way is up?

1

The last thing I recall before things went black involved someone screaming. I can't be sure if the screams came from me, a woman, a man or the tyres of the bus they say hit me full on. I'd been listening to Amy Winehouse on my phone.

I've been told life goes *back to black* for everybody and to not read anything into what happened. I'd expected a white light, a tunnel lined by angels and a benevolent bloke with a beard ready to beckon me through gates. And that's pretty much what I say by way of an icebreaker to the guy who goes through my bag and checks for liquids, explosives, and sharp instruments.

'If I could earn money for every time someone said that,' he mutters without looking up.'Please move along, you're holding up the queue.'

Another popular misconception about death is that your life flashes before your eyes. You get to revisit significant moments. Things like your mother's face when you came out, the day you wet yourself at school, your first orgasm. It doesn't.

I can sum the entire experience up as screaming and darkness.

I'm given a leaflet: Frequently Asked Questions to explain that flashbacks only happen to those whose heart stops beating for at least two seconds. This makes them more grateful when the blood pumps again. An opportunity to look back over life turns them into nicer people.

Deprived of the white light and rapid-fire home movie, all I'm left with is a hazy sense of frustration, and a list of unfinished business: Who'll feed my fish? Why didn't I tell Roy to quit with the flirting? What happens when Tesco try to deliver and nobody's home?

And whether my library card is enough to confirm my identity. I don't much care for a stranger having to prod around in my mouth to establish identification through dental records. I'm not convinced my dentist keeps excellent records. He always looks surprised when I turn up for appointments. And anyway, if they can't identify my body, how will they find the right dentist?

I sound blasé. Like dying doesn't matter, as if I don't care about being mown down in my prime. Truth be told, I'm wrecked, but some girl told me if the people in charge see you get weepy, they whisk you away to a side room with a counsellor. She'd already made that mistake. We had a lot in common. A bus hit me, and she'd thrown herself under a train.

'I was done with everything,' she said with a vague twitch. 'Just didn't want to go on.'

She was one of the most beautiful women I'd ever seen. Tall, slim and delicate. Chestnut hair that covered her shoulders and a flawless milky skin.

'Did you leave anyone behind?' she said.

'My mother is still alive, and I live with my partner.'

'Boy or girl?'

'Boy.'

'I can always tell.'

That's where the conversation ended. I was busy coming to terms with being dead and in no mood for small talk.

* * *

An efficient guy with a clipboard directs me through double doors, and into a hall that reminds me of school. Lined in wood, smelling of gravy and lacking in joy. Rows of plastic chairs fill. Someone has given me a piece of paper stamped with the number sixteen, and I wander to the front of the hall, searching for numbers and empty seats. A guy about my age does the same.

'This is insane,' he says. 'Any idea where to find sixteen?'

'That's my number, too.'

'Oh, right?' He looks at me. 'How did you die?'

'Hit by a bus, you?'

'Heart attack.'

'You're not old enough.'

We cut our conversation short as a door to the left of a raised dais opens and a middle-aged woman with a grey bob, drab suit and brogues makes her way over to a rostrum. She blows twice into a microphone.

'Ladies and gentlemen, welcome to the afterlife,' she says. 'My name is Stella Grainger, Customer Satisfaction Manager. We're circulating leaflets. Take one and pass the rest on. It's all paperwork today, but *everything* is necessary. You need to read *everything* we share and understand it.'

A girl raises her hand. She looks too young to be here. Early teens with soulful, sad almond eyes that scream discontent and she's painfully thin.

Stella ignores this intrusion and goes on.

'You'll be picking up your ID cards. You must keep these with you at all times. Please double check and make sure that *everything* on your card is correct.'

She has this verbal tic that causes her to stress the word *everything*, stretching each syllable like the word matters more than any other in this unknown world.

'If you don't deal with misinformation, the council will restrict your integration allowances. *Everything* is important today, people. Those of you milling, find a seat. I don't care where you sit.'

The young girl keeps her hand in the air, and Stella fixes her with a stare. 'Tomorrow, you'll get the chance to ask questions about *everything*. Today is for listening.'

I half expect the girl to burst into tears, but she doesn't. Instead, her eyes grow black and her face rearranges into what I can only describe as a mask of evil.

Stella tuts. 'Don't bother with the death stares, young lady. In case you haven't yet realised, they won't work on those of us who are already dead,'

The girl looks down at the floor.

'Right, now if we can continue without childish interruptions, I'll try not to keep you. You'll all want to find where your rooms are, so when I call your name, come up, collect your access card and return to your seats. Any issues with your cards, check with one of our Customer Services Agents at the back of the room. These are busy people, you only need to consult a CSA to correct factual inaccuracies. They can't do anything if you hate your photo.'

She reads out names, and I turn to the guy from before. 'Where are you from?'

'Oslo.'

'Your English is superb. No trace of an accent. Did you spend time in the UK?'

He looks baffled. 'I would say the same about your Norwegian.'

We stare at each other, neither sure what to say next.

Stella calls my name and I head for the stage.

'Check the details, inform a CSA if you spot problems, otherwise please return to your seat.'

'I wanted to ask you something.'

'We've set aside ample time for Q&A tomorrow, when we split you into work groups.' She returns to her clipboard. 'Otto Steinberg.'

And so it goes on.

* * *

Stella claps her hands to show she once again needs our attention. 'You all have questions, and my team is on hand to clarify *everything* over the course of the next few days. Today has been a busy day and it would be best to confirm where you'll sleep tonight.'

People peer around.

'You all received a number. May I trust you've held on to the tickets?'

A tall, thin elderly man in thick-rimmed glasses raises his hand. 'I appear to have mislaid mine.'

'Find me afterwards.'

Stella's tone discourages discussion.

'I recall mine said sixteen, though,' he says.

'That's neither here nor there. If we are to get on at all, then you need to learn how to value company property.'

'I thought I'd been given a raffle ticket.'

Stella puts down her clipboard and folds her arms. Even from a distance, I sense flared nostrils. 'A raffle ticket?' she says. 'Do you expect me to countenance the idea that you expected a raffle… in the afterlife?'

The room falls silent.

'Gambler, were you? Fond of a flutter?'

'I don't consider that my habits are your business.'

Stella doesn't rise to the bait, instead her mouth rearranges into a smile. 'Good point,' she says. 'None of my business. None of my business at all.'

The smile fades almost as fast as it formed.

'However, the ticket is very much my business. Ladies and gentlemen, let me make things clear. *Everything* we give you is important. Do you imagine we hand slips of paper out for fun? The numbers dictate which hall you go to for dinner and where you will find your rooms. We follow a system here, people. Without one, we'd encounter chaos.'

The object of Stella's disdain stays on his feet. 'But like I said, I remember the number.'

'And what proof do I have that you're telling the truth? No offence, but you're not all here thanks to endless hours spent reading to the blind.'

An uncomfortable silence sets in.

The man with no number sits with a heavy sigh.

The girl next to me leans in to whisper. 'I've got six. My lucky number.'

Stella is back in charge. 'Everyone, listen up. When I call your number, please stand and make your way out to meet your zone heads.'

One by one, people drift away.

Number six girl squeezes my hand. 'I hope we'll talk again soon.'

She reminds me of a child being left at school, trying to convince both her and me that everything is fine no matter what.

When they call sixteen, I follow others into the corridor where we exchange nervous smiles until a northern voice calls the group to order.

A short squat woman in her early fifties with a basin cut holds up a folded umbrella. 'Number sixteens,' she says. 'Gather round.'

Eleven of us huddle as she runs down names. 'Which one of you is Ben?'

I step forward.

'Anne Williams.' We shake hands and she looks at her list. 'Hit by a bus, not paying attention, blame in doubt.' I'm treated to a perfunctory smile, and she glances around, ever-so-slightly cross. 'I'm missing someone. Don't say one of my boys is already in trouble with the boss.'

She heads back into the hall, returning minutes later with the guy who lost his ticket.

'Come along number sixteens,' she says with two clicks of her tongue. 'Time for dinner.'

We follow her down a white corridor, and she maintains a running commentary. 'It's all good stuff, but steer clear of the spotted dick, cook goes heavy on the suet. I often order soup and a sandwich. Killer tip, the Coronation Chicken is to die for.'

She stops and laughs.

'That's my afterlife joke. You've been through *that* already.'

In the dining hall, lost souls mill, holding red plastic trays.

'Two by two, please,' Anne orders. 'Newbies should stick together.'

I partner up with the lost ticket guy

'Malcolm,' he introduces himself.

'Ben.'

'Did they tell you they expect us to work for our keep?'

'But we're dead.'

'Killed ourselves.'

'What?'

'We caused our own deaths.'

'A bus hit me. I didn't hear the thing coming. How is that my fault?'

'Listening to music?'

I nod.

'Then they'll class the incident as your fault.'

'That's not fair.'

Malcolm is only the messenger, but this new rule leaves me with an overwhelming sense of being diddled.

'Doesn't matter to them whether you swallowed a bucket of pills with a bottle of whisky or slipped off a chair because you grew too idle to get the ladder to change a lightbulb. In their eyes, any accident is your fault, so you're obliged to work.'

He picks up a tray.

'Is that how you died?' I say. 'Falling off a chair?'

'Not exactly,' he says and takes a slice of pork pie.

I've avoided dwelling on what appears to be happening. Part of me remains convinced this is a mad but entertaining dream.

'Am I dead?' I say.

'Of course you are, you silly fucker, now move along, you're holding up the queue.'

My mouth goes dry and my stomach flips. I might be sick and lean on a counter for support. Anne bustles over, her face full of worry. I can't make out a single word. I hit the floor. Things go dark again.

2

I wake in a white room, wrapped in white sheets surrounded by white curtains.

'How are you?' A soft voice asks. 'You suffered with a funny turn. Death gets people that way.'

I try to sit up, but can't move. Someone has fastened tight belts around my head, my chest, my legs, my arms. Who'd do that? A trickle of alarm radiates through me. 'What's going on? Where am I?'

'Hush now. Lie still a while.'

It's a woman's voice that sounds to mean no harm. 'You fell, and we have to be sure you didn't do yourself any damage.'

'But I'm dead, how can I do myself more damage?'

'They all ask that. You'd be surprised. Just because you've come through one thing, you're not invincible.'

'So I could die again?'

'No, don't be silly. This is the afterlife. Where else is there to go?'

'So why *am* I here?'

'You need to lie still and wait. Doctor will be in to see you. If everything is fine, you can return to your group this evening.'

'But I'm dead.' My voice grows louder from frustration.

'And I suppose you'd be happy to spend the afterlife hobbling round on a broken leg?'

'I don't understand.'

'You might well be dead, it doesn't mean you can't hurt yourself.'

The nurse sits on a white chair. 'How on earth would I earn a living if everyone healed themselves?'

A door opens, and in walks the most handsome man I've ever seen. His soft blue eyes transmit compassion. A floppy dark fringe falls across a tanned face.

'They tell me you fell, Ben,' he says. 'I'm Doctor Parsons, but call me Martin. If it's OK with you, I'll do a few tests to make sure of no lasting damage, and if everything is fine, you'll be on your way.'

He shines lights into my eyes and ears, listens to my heart and takes my blood pressure. He taps limbs and checks readings. And pronounces me fit to leave.

'If you get a headache in the next twenty-four hours, you must come back. Your group leader knows how to find me.' He hands over a slip of paper. 'Give this to the desk on the way out to make sure we're paid.'

I do as he says, though, can't ignore a nagging worry. It's the second mention today of payment. Where is this money coming from? Are they somehow tapping into bank accounts to retrieve funds left behind? My father used to say there were no pockets in shrouds. Was he wrong all this time?

Thinking about Dad makes me wonder if I might get to see him again. What with us both being dead, and all. He surrendered to aggressive cancer five years back while I sat with Mum watching as a grey man gasped for air in a hospital bed. The doctors took us aside and asked what to do if his heart stopped beating. Neither she nor I hesitated. Let him go, we said, and then held each other, fearful of judgement.

By the time I reach the reception, a hundred questions whirl around my head, and I hand the paper to a smiling woman who nods towards the door.

Anne Williams waits.

'Back from the wars,' she says and clasps horrified fingers to her mouth. 'No offence to anyone who fought in a war.'

She leans in to whisper. 'You need to be *so* careful up here.'

***

A taxi drops us outside a bland concrete and glass building. Red-tiled steps lead to revolving doors and into a foyer bathed in orange light. A security guard waves. A buzzer sounds and a glass screen slides aside to reveal three lift doors.

Anne pushes the button, and we wait. And wait. And wait.

'These lifts get worse,' she says.

'I hope I haven't put you to any trouble. This death thing is new to me. Until yesterday, I was going about my business, thinking I'd got years left.'

Anne shakes her head. 'You're borderline. Still waiting for the paperwork to come through from upstairs. That's why they've allocated you to my group.'

'I don't understand.'

'Group sixteen, love. They call us the Biddies. B.I.D. Blame In Doubt.'

'Blame?'

'I shouldn't be telling you all this. Stella is super strict about only providing information during scheduled sessions. Outside those hours, we're not supposed to discuss matters. But seeing as you missed the Q&A this evening, I'll make an exception.'

The lift arrives, and we get in.

'When a person dies, they land up here. In most cases. Except those that go to *the other place*.'

I nod and she carries on.

'You can imagine that as time has gone on, things grew crowded. Time was, you'd die, come in, have a cup of tea, collect a pamphlet and go about your business. The afterlife council looked after us. We worked hard and nobody got anything for nothing, but keep your head down and do your best, and you'd get your own house and manage fine. It was all very dignified, from what I can gather. Then the new lot got in.'

Her voice becomes a whisper. 'New ideas, new values. I remember when they took charge. Everybody sang and danced in the streets. They'd all grown fed up of the old lot and their empty promises. Change hung in the air, and this new bunch promised everyone a fair deal. They said those who died of natural causes deserved better treatment than people who caused their own death. We fell for it hook, line and sinker. It sounded fair on paper. Illegals... people who jumped the queue and got here before their time *should* work. It wasn't long before the council clamped down. At one point, if you'd worked all your life before you passed, you could expect to spend the afterlife relaxing and meeting old friends. Now, unless you die of natural causes, they make you pay. First, they started on those who couldn't cope with living. The bridge jumpers and pill-poppers. Then it was the smokers. The overweight. It makes you wonder who'll be next.'

The lift doors open and a man and a woman with a small child get in. When they step back out a few floors later, Anne carries on.

'Things got worse when they sent all the boat people up. That's when the council started a formal induction programme. Except they tried to do everything on a shoestring. You'd only need a bomb or a school shooting, and they ran us ragged. Imagine what it was like on 9/11 or during Corona. So, you're with me. Everyone goes through basic training and it's my role to make sure you understand your responsibilities as a citizen of the afterlife. The system will assign a job and expect you to perform to the best of your ability during the hours prescribed for your function. As far as possible, you'll do something that maximises your existing skills.'

She stops and studies my face. 'I've a mind like a sieve, what did you do when alive?'

'I wrote software.'

'Oh splendid. Definite lack of your sort up here. Computers are relatively new in the grand scheme of things. Most of the people who understand the hardcore stuff are still young and apart from the odd Japanese mass suicide, there's a skills shortage.'

'Not all bad news then?' I say, not without a hint of sarcasm, something she picks up on.

'Well, that is just the thing, Ben. Dying might not be what either of us planned on doing, but we're stuck with it. Look on the bright side, you're a Biddy.'

'Blame in doubt,' I say.

'If they find you're not to blame for your death, you'll be one of the privileged few and get a house with fitted carpets, a car in the drive and money every week.'

The lift doors open. My head spins from information overload.

'I've condensed things and you'll have questions, but it's late and I need my beauty sleep, even if you don't.'

She leads me down yet another corridor and stops outside a door where an engraved plate reads "Ben Walker. Malcolm Hutty."

'This is you. Use your card to get in, like in a hotel. Try not to wake Malcolm. After what he drank at dinner, I suspect he'll be asleep.' She chuckles to herself. 'He's quite a character, that one. Stella's gunning for him. Mind you, he'll give as good as he gets.'

'I want to learn,' I say.

She places a finger on my lips. 'You will, petal. But don't go worrying about that now. You've got all the time going. Literally. I'll find you after breakfast tomorrow for class and I'm sure I'll be able to answer some of your questions then.'

'I miss Gary.'

From the day we first met, Gary and I have been inseparable. We've never spent longer than 24 hours apart. Why have I not given him a second thought in amongst everything that happened? Even when that girl asked earlier, I let him slip from my mind.

'Who is Gary?' Anne says.

'My boyfriend.'

'Oh, I see.' She looks far less sympathetic, and I assume Anne has little time for the gays. 'Tell me if you continue to feel this way.'

I'm confused. 'You expect me to speak up if I continue to miss someone I love?'

'Yes, if you have extended feelings like this.'

She sounds worried.

'I love him.'

'You *loved* him, petal. Now you're gone. Let him go. If you carry on loving him, he'll never get over you. That's the way it goes. You want him to have a life of his own?'

Tears prickle my eyes. 'I don't want to stop loving him.'

'You have to Ben, for your sake as much as his. Now take a deep breath. Trust me.'

I do as she says, and Anne watches, encouraging me to take a second deep breath. To my surprise, as I let the air back out, the sharpness passes and Gary is no longer anything but a soft warm glow in my heart.

'Better?' she asks.

'Better,' I confirm, and she looks relieved.

'Gary will be fine now. He *knows* you loved him. The letting go is always the hardest part.'

Inside the room, there's a tiny desk and two doors. One with my name that opens when I swipe my ID card, furnished with a bed, a narrow desk and two bookcases stacked with favourite books and a small picture frame filled with images of Mum, Dad, Gary and our dog Banjo. I stare for a while, before curling up on the pillow, fully clothed, and expect sadness, but tears refuse to come. Instead, I'm overcome by the most incredible sense of calm and, soon enough, sleep.

3

They serve breakfast in the same enormous hall where I fainted the previous evening. I make my way to the lift alone. Malcolm has gone missing. I knocked on his door. He didn't answer.

From overflowing counters, I help myself to tea and toast and wonder how all those smug religious types will react when they discover the afterlife is little more than a running buffet. Someone touches my arm. The Norwegian guy from yesterday, holding a tray loaded with food. 'You must be hungry.'

I allow a smile. 'I could eat a scabby horse.'

'Is that an old Norwegian proverb?'

'Never heard it before.'

We make our way through the hall and bag a table near a window. Outside, a beautiful waterfall cascades onto rocks where small children sit and watch.

'They'll get wet, I wonder where their parents are?' I say.

'Who?'

'The kids by the waterfall.'

'What waterfall?'

I point with my knife.

'Oh,' he says. 'So you see a waterfall?'

'Don't you?'

'I see snow. Kilometres of snow, nothing but snow, pure, white and peaceful.' He closes her eyes and smiles. 'They explained last night. The other side of these windows is the world we *want*. In reality, there isn't anything outside. We're sixty floors up.'

'How do *they* know what we want?'

'They just do,' he says. 'Isn't that wonderful?'

I'm not so sure. Everything is so intrusive, like someone waded into my head and helped themselves.

'You most likely ticked a box,' he says. 'Anne said everyone does. They hide the afterlife clause in Apple's terms and conditions.'

We eat in silence, interrupted only by Malcolm, who tracks me down and pulls up a chair. 'I never heard you come in, old chap.'

'I stayed up late.'
'Oh well, never mind. Anne says we should all meet on the seventh floor.'
'Don't suppose you'd lead the way?'

* * *

Anne has changed into a smart blouse and pleated skirt and looks more like a Girl Scout leader than someone charged with inducting the deceased to a long and happy afterlife.
'Good morning campers,' she says. 'Everyone sleep well?'
Mumbled greetings and nods are enough, she herds us towards the lift.
'Time to start work. Two by two.'
She tells Malcolm and me to get out at floor ninety-five.
'Go to the desk and ask for Gretchen. She's a trooper. You'll have a ball.'
Gretchen turns out to be a tall black woman who looks in need of sleep.
'You'll have a fucking ball,' she says and hands us overalls.
We're dressed in white as she opens a door leading into what looks like a vast warehouse. The noise is incredible. Like a hundred school kids, running their fingers down blackboards.
'What the hell is that?' Malcolm asks.
'Soundtrack.' Gretchen doles out ear protectors. 'Keep these on or the noise will drive you insane.'
We follow her, but even with thick plastic domes over each ear I make out babies crying, vicious dogs barking, lairy football chants and a medley of Eurovision winners.
'What do you do here?' I say.
'We make soundtracks.'
'For who?'
'We only have one customer.' Gretchen stops and grins. 'The place downstairs.'
'We're making soundtracks for hell?' I ask, and she nods. 'Outsourcing is a dirty job, but somebody has to do it.'
We're handed dental drills and blocks of limestone. 'Away you go, aisle six,

they're expecting you.'

'This is fucking mad,' laughs Malcolm. 'We're recording the soundtrack to hell.'

'Rather this than Abba on a loop tape.'

'Don't you gays love Abba?'

'They've a lot to answer for.'

* * *

It's a long day drilling into limestone and messy work. But not as unpleasant as you might imagine. We're hooked up to machines piping music that changes as you think of something new, and fed cream cakes, meat pies and milk shakes.

'I could get used to this,' Malcolm says as we get changed.

'Hang on,' I say. 'Did someone wash your clothes? Mine are like new.'

'Fuck me,' Malcolm laughs. 'Should have shot myself sooner.'

He goes ahead, and all I can wonder is what went so wrong he needed to put a gun to his head and pull the trigger? Over dinner, I get my answer.

'The bank repossessed my house, and I wrote a letter and blew my brains out in front of one of their pretty little cashiers.'

'Why would you do that?' asks the girl to my right.

Her name is Jennifer. She jumped from the balcony of a high rise when social services took away her baby.

Malcolm shrugs. 'I wanted to make them understand how much they hurt me.'

'But what about that poor girl?'

'And what about the poor fucker who scraped *you* up off the floor?'

She looks mortified.

'And what about that poor kiddie of yours?' he continues. 'What they gonna tell the little runt when he asks what happened to his mother? Wouldn't surprise me if he wants revenge on the sods that took away his mammy. He'll get a gun like mine, but he won't point the thing at the right person, and end up rotting in a cell, waiting to fucking die.'

'Language,' Anne reprimands. 'We're not in the other place.'

Jennifer's eyes turn bright red, but she says nothing, and plays with her food.

'You need to apologise,' I say to Malcolm.

He laughs. 'The sanctimonious cunt.'

Anne takes me aside after dinner. 'You can't make moral judgments. You missed the initiation briefing, so this time, we'll let your transgression go. It's a strict rule, and if you break rules…'

'So Malcolm gets to say what he likes, even though he hurt that poor girl's feelings?'

'That's the downside of blame,' Anne says. 'You learn to put up with a lot of crap.'

That evening, Malcolm sulks off to bed early, but only after telling me I'm a good bloke and promising to apologise to Jennifer.

'I'm not sure you should,' I say.

Malcolm snorts. 'This place is fucking mental, mate.'

* * *

Four days later and the weekend comes.

'We don't have to work?' I ask Anne.

'Two days off,' she confirms. 'Do what you want. Go to the beach, swim in a lake, climb a mountain. Report to the leisure pods and the rest is down to you.'

The leisure pods resemble tanning booths. You're handed goggles and told to step inside and imagine what you want to do.

At first, I'm in a meadow, surrounded by trees, watching friends enjoy a picnic. I want to join in, but as I approach, something lifts me away.

Suddenly, I'm on a beach. Alone. Miles from anywhere with the sea lapping. I lie down and music plays. The sun is hot, but my skin doesn't burn, and I'm not hungry or thirsty. I rest and feel immortal.

When I wake, I'm dressed in the most wonderful stylish clothes, sipping cocktails in a tiny bar, overlooking New York listening to the best music ever.

Kirsty MacColl is on stage, strumming a guitar and engaging the crowd in banter. New songs. A swirl of new melodies.

'It's time to go,' says the barman. 'Time you got home.'

I don't need telling twice. I've fast picked up on how to follow orders in the afterlife. You question nothing.

* * *

'They've decided,' Anne says as I step into the lift on Monday morning.

'Who?'

'The people in charge.' The look on her face tells me she doesn't have good news. 'I'm sorry, love. You do this next bit on your own.'

The door closes to darkness, and I'm falling.

Air rushes past and I flail for something to hold on to.

The walls around grow hotter and hotter, then colder, and the darkness turns back to light.

'He's opening his eyes,' a voice cries.

Is that Gary? Someone holds my hand and squeezes my wrist. I can't move but force open an eye. The light fades, then bursts back. Blurred faces, mixed voices. Everything hurts so much.

'You stupid sod,' Gary says. 'You gave us such a scare.'

I want to speak, but my tongue stays glued to the roof of my mouth.

* * *

I throw the ball and Banjo lets it bounce. He's not interested in such things. Not with rabbits to hunt or magpies to bark away. Gary laughs and gives chase. Down the hill and back again.

Far, far away I pick up on Anne's voice.

'Be happy. Stay happy.'

About time

Cake. She has to have cake. For an entire week, Anna walked past the window of *Truly Scrumptious*, averting her eyes.

Last night, she had two bowls of cabbage soup and a bifidus yoghurt. Then later, infused with Zen-like smugness, she ran a hot bath and lit candles. Surrounded by expensive foam, she congratulated herself on a week of self-control.

At 3 am, she woke, went downstairs, and poured an entire bag of oven chips onto a baking tray.

'Morning Anna,' Glenda said, looking up from arranging éclairs on a tray. 'Haven't seen you all week. Have you been away? Anywhere nice?'

She shook her head. Words were the least of her concerns. She wanted one of the blueberry muffins piled up behind the glass.

'We've got some lovely carrot cake. Baked it myself.' Glenda wiped her hands and placed the éclairs on the counter within reach. Anna could smell the bitter dark chocolate topping.

'I'll take a plain scone,' she forced herself to say.

Glenda's face said it all. 'Just a scone?'

'Just a scone.'

'But you'll have clotted cream and jam? Strawberry jam.'

'I'm on a diet,' Anna said.

Glenda's face changed. 'You? On a diet?' She didn't add 'you don't need to lose weight'. Her face said 'about time.'

'I'm trying to slim down for my holiday.'

'Well, each to their own.' Glenda put the single miserable-looking scone into a brown-paper bag. 'As long as you're doing it for you, not for some bloke.'

'As if.'

Anna managed a smile.

Later that morning, Anna sees him across the room. He's leaning over Lesley Fowler's desk. Skinny Lesley. She's doing that giggly thing she does when there's a good-looking bloke within flirting distance. He looks up, smiles at Anna and does a goofy wave. She does the same back. He mimes drinking. She nods. So they've made a date.

Except it isn't a date. Ben is her best friend.

'Lunch orders.'

Anna looks up to find Lesley smiling. 'I've got leftovers,' she lies.

'Suit yourself. I'm going to Bert's.'

Anna pictures apple pie. Oozing pastry, dusted with cinnamon. Bert's do the best pie in town. Everyone knows it.

'Get me a salad,' she says.

'Just a salad?'

'Plain green, no dressing.'

'Are you on a diet?'

'Sort of. Not really. Well, a bit. Just watching my carb intake.'

There's that look again. 'About time.'

At five, Anna switches off her computer, shrugs on her jacket and goes to find Ben. Together they head for the next-door pub. He orders bitter. She has lager. Pints. They find a table in the corner and collapse into soft leather armchairs.

'I'm thinking of asking Lesley out,' Ben says.

'Oh?'

'Am I batting out of my league?'

Out of his league? Is Ben mad? He's tall, slim with matinee idol looks.

'You're probably too good for her,' she says, taking a slug of her drink.

'What makes you say that?'

'Lesley's a nice person,' Anna lies, 'and I really like her.' She'll go to hell for adding one untruth to another.

'But?'

'But nothing. Ask her out. You two look good together.'

Ben downs what's left of his drink and goes to the bar. Anna watches him, wondering where it all went wrong. First day in the job, he was appointed her mentor. He showed her round and took her to lunch, insisting she order whatever she wanted, and laughing when she suggested two deserts over a main course. Two weeks later he'd asked her for a drink, then took her to dinner. For a while, it looked like they might become an item. But instead, they drifted into friendship. Meeting up after work to laugh and gossip.

'I got you some nuts,' Ben says as he sits down.

'Oh, right. Thanks, but I'm trying to lose weight.'

She studies his face, waiting for the 'about time' look.

'Why?' he asks.

'Why what?'

'Why are you trying to lose weight? Is there a man involved?'

Anna folds her arms.

'Why can't I do something for myself? Why does it always have to be for someone else? Why does everyone assume I'm doing it for a man?'

Ben's face changes.

'Sorry.' He looks away and mutters something.

'What?'

He shakes his head.

'Go on. Tell me what you just said.'

'OK.' Ben takes a deep breath. 'What I hate about you is that you never tell people the truth. You say what you think they want to hear. You spend half your life tip-toeing around when the worst thing that could ever happen is that someone doesn't like you.'

'Wow,' Anna says. 'Where did this all come from?'

He's not done. All the time he's addressing the floor, not looking her in the eyes.

'And all that would be fine, if just for once, you'd stop thinking about what others want and...'

'And what?'

'Do what you want. Put yourself first.'
'I am doing what I want. I'm losing weight for me.'
'But I like you as you are.'
'Bully for you. Shame everyone else sees this big fat lump.'
Ben looks up. 'Is that what you think?'
Anna nods. Here it is, she thinks.
The 'about time' face.
The kiss, when it happens, takes them both by surprise.
The next morning, their eyes open at almost the same time. She doesn't feel awkward; it feels right.
'Did you mean what you said?' she asked.
He nodded. 'About time,' he'd said. 'About time.'

First published as part of '100 Stories for Haiti', March 2010

Home

I'm so glad your friends have promised to come. I've hunted high and low for a cake shaped like a racing car. I know they make them; I saw one on the telly. I even thought of trying to bake one myself and ice it up, but last time I did that, the sponges came out like biscuits. I suggested putting them out for the birds, but your father said if they ate my cake, they'd never get off the ground again. He laughed about how it was a good job he didn't marry me for my cooking. I said something about the crooked shelves in the pantry, but he pretended not to hear.

It reminded me of that time I wanted him to touch up the skirting board in your old room; I nagged night and day until he did it, even then he somehow got paint on the carpet, so I had to move that chest of drawers you used to keep your Blue Peter annuals in over it. It's never looked good there. Anyway, the long and short of it is that I couldn't find the cake I wanted, so I settled for one done up like a football.

I've made egg sandwiches and sausage rolls. I dare say they'll all end up trodden into the carpet, but you can't not offer them, can you? I've put chunks of cheese and pineapple onto sticks and stuck them into a foil-wrapped half cabbage. It isn't a buffet without a cheese hedgehog.

You can go sing for vol-au-vents, last time I did them I followed the recipe perfectly, but your father said they tasted like cardboard cases filled with wallpaper paste and refused to touch them.

You had to run out and get fish and chips.

I never heard the last of it. He still reckons he's funny by mentioning it whenever we have guests round. "Don't overlook the vol-au-vents, Mary," he says, and then tells everyone about how I misinterpreted the recipe and put in two tablespoons of corn flour and not two teaspoons. They sell them ready-made, but all the same…

For drinks I was stumped.

When little, you were a fiend for blackcurrant. But you're a big lad now and so I decided I'd put out fruit juice and few cans of lager for the grown-ups.

I'm hoping your Uncle Patrick doesn't drink too much and get out his mouth organ, not that he demands prompting. Some of those songs he sang last Christmas were blue.

A few of the ladies from the church said they'd pop their heads in, so I must keep my eye on him.

Last night I looked through old photos. I got the albums down from the top of the wardrobe in your room. I felt guilty though; they were covered in cobwebs.

It's all very well keeping a shrine, it still calls for a dusting now and again. I've let things go since that upset with my hip. It doesn't do to keep climbing on chairs. Your father reckons he'll report me to the health visitor. Not that she'd be bothered. She's hardly here five seconds.

The other morning she said, 'What's it to be, a hot meal or a shower?'

I stared at her like she might be mad.

'You can't have both,' she said. 'There's a budget.'

I settled for the shower. It hurts to raise my arms up, and she knows how to do it right.

We had bread and butter for lunch with ham.

I remember your tenth birthday. We had a huge party in the back garden. All your friends showed up. I'm not sure whether to blame the trifle or the party games, but I spent half the afternoon hosing down the steps and scraping up sick.

Kids these days don't play games, though. They want iPods and you tubes. I asked the lad in Tesco what might be suitable for a party and he looked at me gone out.

They printed your picture in the paper when the court passed sentence. I came down to take in the milk and there were people camping in our front hedge. I presume this must be what Joan Collins goes through.

It hardly seemed fair when they moved you to Manchester. Isn't the idea to keep families together? It put a burden on your father. Sid blamed me and we had this one almighty row when he said if I hadn't *wrapped you up in cotton wool* you wouldn't be in the mess you were.

To hear him talk, the best way to bring up your kids was to refuse them everything and never show them any tenderness.

His mother was hardly a good example. She was all bones and sharp corners, a miserable little mouth and watery cold eyes. I'd rather have my method any day of the week.

* * *

After Sid died, I was lonely. The doctor put me on pills and recommended therapy. Like Americans have, but less fancy. I sat in a brown room with a woman called Hilary. She spoke, and I listened. I'm positive they meant it to be the other way round.

The long and short, according to Hilary, was that I should get out more. That was why I got lonely. I needed more friends.

I could have told her that.

Hilary was insistent that I join a group for newly bereaved mothers. She gave me a pamphlet; it was dull reading.

I took my chances with the Church of England.

They were having a bake sale, so I popped in.

Like anything with the church, they make you sit through a service before you get to the decent stuff. The vicar was new. She was talking about how we had to take in more refugees. I sat at the back and listened.

Over scones and tea, some ladies recognised me from the papers and I suppose they took pity. They invited me to their houses for coffee. They were a friendly group. Turned out we had more in common than I could have expected.

Everyone wanted to know about you.

Their kids had all flown the nest too. One or two had lost their husbands; one or two said they wished they could lose them.

It's just something you say.

They've been so helpful.

* * *

Notice might have been nice, but you've never been the predictable sort, have you? Doreen suggested having the vicar say a few words, I said you weren't religious and it might look odd if she spouted on about God. Not everyone believes. I gave in and phoned her, but she's pre-booked to open a fete at the big school, so you needn't worry.

I told Doreen, and she said something about it perhaps being for the best, anyway.

I've no idea what to wear. With all this food about, it has to be practical. I know I look good in that black skirt I got for Christmas from your sister, but it shows every mark. Speaking of Chrissie, she rang to say she wouldn't be able to make it. Typical Chrissie, she's busy putting together a big presentation for work. Still, you two never saw eye to eye.

I'll probably wear that blue dress your father got me for my birthday three years ago. I wore that time in Manchester and you told me I looked nice.

* * *

I've still no idea when you plan on getting here. Ever since you moved back down to London, I've breathed easier. It used to be quite the hike to come up north. A widow's pension doesn't go far. When you said you would be three bus rides away, it lifted a weight off my mind.

That number 42 isn't what it was. I waited nearly half an hour for one the last time, and then two came along at once. The driver kept stopping and starting.

I hope the cake isn't too childish.

* * *

When I phoned Chrissie to tell her you were coming home, she didn't sound shocked. She said one way, or another it was bound to happen one day. If I'm honest, in the back of my mind I knew she was right. The thing is, I never thought it would happen yet. They were supposed to look after you.

When the governor called me and asked me to come down, I told myself you'd been up to your old tricks. How many times did I get summoned to your school?

They sent a car round, and I got chatting to the driver. His name was Harry. He had a son too. About your age. Only Harry's lad isn't in prison, he manages a big department store up west.

The governor was waiting in that bit where they pat you down and ask if you're trying to smuggle stuff in. I held out my handbag and coat, but she waved them away. She wasn't wearing her usual smart blouse and jacket. She looked like she'd got out of bed and thrown on the first things she could find.

We went to her office, and it was nicer than I expected. She grows herbs in tin cans. I told her I can never get those pots of basil to live longer than two days.

Someone brought me a cup of tea.

I remember her talking and talking.

She told me what had happened.

'How did this happen?' I asked her. 'I thought you were keeping an eye on him. After what they put in the paper, I thought he was being watched?'

She said nobody knew how you got hold of the belt. They took yours away, and your shoelaces. She said they couldn't tell me any more, as there was to be an enquiry and it would be up to the lawyers to say who was to blame. They asked if I'd like to speak to a counsellor.

HOME

'No, I'd like to speak to my son and explain to him how I still love him,' I said.

* * *

I didn't cry in front of them. I'm not that sort. I waited until I got home. Then I made myself another cup of tea and sat down. I put on the telly.

I suppose the tears must have stopped, eventually. I can't remember when. Now I'm numb around the edges and it's only organising this little get together for you that has kept me going.

I hope you'll like it.

When they asked me if I wanted to bring you home first, I didn't hesitate. It's what I've always dreamed of. To have you here and tell you it will all be OK. Protect you from the wagging tongues and the made-up minds. They didn't know you. Now they never can. As Sid would say, you're no angel.

You were my angel.

Now it seems I'm the one they're watching. Strangers keep checking up, making sure I'm all right. Everyone. The ladies from church. The people in my street. Probably whoever smeared dog dirt on the front door last week.

They all keep asking if there's anything they can do.

I'm the one they pity, not you.

At least my life isn't lonely, so I've you to thank for that.

First Published in 2008 as part of 'Great Short Stories', a compilation by new writers.

The blackbird

The sound of dishes being stacked on shelves signals the end of early morning peace and quiet. Ever since we moved to this house, I've enjoyed the first few hours of the day alone with my thoughts.

The blackbird on the lawn cocks his head to the ground, listens and lunges to grab a worm. He swallows it whole.

We catch each other's eye.

'It's OK, I won't tell anyone. You go about your business.'

This house wasn't my idea. I was happy in Vicarage Road.

* * *

'There's neither of us getting any younger,' Anne announced one morning as she larded butter onto white sliced bread. 'And unless they can perform miracles and move you up the waiting list, that hip of yours will cause problems. You've trouble enough with the stairs as it is and I refuse to have one of those chair lifts, I don't want people thinking we're old.'

She picked up the morning paper.

I said nothing, and just carried on reading about how to get rose bushes ready for winter. The secret is a good handful of blood, fish and bone. Keep an eye on new growths before they get out of hand.

Susan is good at making sure things never get out of hand.

It's why I married her.

'Got a good head on her shoulders that one,' Mother said.

We told no one she was two months gone. That was a bridge to cross when we reached it. Only we never did. One Sunday teatime, she took bad, collapsed in the front room and hit her head on the fireplace.

She called losing the kiddie a blessing in disguise. It saved having to have *an awkward conversation.*

* * *

She's finished in the kitchen and come into the living room.

'You never listened to a word I said before, why should it be any different now?'

She tidies away a plate left on the coffee table from last night.

'Dave and Marie are coming round for supper tonight. They want to see you. God knows why.'

* * *

We never had *supper* in Vicarage Road. We had our tea. Chop and chips, stew with dumplings. A nice bit of steak on a Friday. All at the table, not like now, eaten from trays balanced on knees in front of 'Eggheads'.

We had real friends in Vicarage Road.

Folk looked out for each other.

It wasn't a palace, but it had a heart. Not like this concrete box with its feature fireplace and triple-glazed windows.

Susan folds a magazine and lays it on the sofa. The sofa I bought in the closing down sale at Hale's. She'd had her eye on it for months. Kept a picture of it pinned on the kitchen cupboard.

'When we win the pools, this is what I'm buying,' she used to say.

I put notes in vases and hid pound coins in socks.

Her face was a picture the day it got delivered.

How was I to know she wanted it in blue?

I'm surprised it didn't end up wrapped in black plastic at the end of the hall earmarked for church jumble. Between her and her friends, she keeps that place running. Arranging flowers, baking cakes, polishing pews. And the vicar still has the nerve to pass a plate round on Sunday.

'He ought to pay you,' I said once.

'Wait until you get to the Pearly Gates,' she sniffed. 'You'll find your name is down for the other place.'

I ran into the vicar outside the chemists. I'd been in to pick up tablets for gout. He nodded at my bag.

'Something to make that lovely wife of yours even more beautiful?'

'It's for my foot if you must know.'

'That lovely wife of your keeping you on your toes, is she?'

I pretended to laugh, and he got into his double-parked Mondeo.

* * *

She keeps looking out of the window and I wonder what's wrong.

'That bloody blackbird,' she says. 'He's making a mess of my borders. I might have to get a cat.'

I'm allergic to cats, but she knows that.

'We should have moved here years ago,' she says. 'Why we put up with that dump is beyond me. Retirement is the time for living, not coping.'

* * *

That night before we flitted our friends threw a party. For once, Susan seemed willing to smile without me having to coax the joy out. She even got up and danced with Big Larry. She was a different woman.

'Would you do me the honour of this dance,' Larry put on a posh voice.

We were only in the snug of the Holly Bush, but when they put Brotherhood of Man on the jukebox, she got up.

She'd always been a fan of the Eurovision Song Contest.

She knew all the words and the dance moves. There were four of them in a row, all laughing and trying to keep up with each other. Susan, Big Larry, Big Larry's wife Enid and Bridie from the flower shop.

I clapped along. We all clapped. That was a glorious night. She even let me have a couple of cigarettes without tutting.

You know what, Alfred, she's not so bad, I thought to myself. Look at her now.

Isn't that the woman you married, isn't that the girl you fell in love with?

It's amazing what three pints of mixed does for your judgement.

The van turned up the morning after to take away our things. Two lads, barely out of nappies armed with rolls of sticky tape and bubble wrap. They packed our life into boxes and sealed it away, numbering each and writing details on a piece of paper. They gave me a copy.

'An inventory', they called it.

In my day, it would have been a list.

Why do people have to go inventing extra words when we've already got perfectly good ones?

I had to sign to say everything was in order and it felt strange, like I was signing away my life, putting it all into boxes and sending it on its way.

Susan went ahead, armed with a bottle of bleach, a tin of Pledge and six dozen dusters.

After they left, I sat on the floor and looked around our empty back room. At the marks on the walls pictures had been. Susan blamed my smoking.

When we moved in, we didn't have the money for underlay and used copies of the Express and Star. I peeled one away and read about Cliff Richard opening a supermarket in Netherton. Those were the days when a supermarket was something special.

Why did I stand by and let her crush me? We never used to be like this. We used to go dancing. We used to laugh.

* * *

I watch her now with a jar of vinegar and newspaper as she rubs away at the windows. Still in that pink striped housecoat with buttons that barely meet.

The last time she let me out was when I went to get milk. She said I was getting under her feet.

'What choice do I have? You know what the doctor said.'

'Fresh air might do you good.'

I didn't need telling twice. I was glad of the break.

I bought myself ten Bensons and a lottery ticket and sat on a bench near the swings, smoking a forbidden fag.

'Gis a fake, mister.'

The lad stood in front of me couldn't have been more than twelve. Curly brown hair, blue eyes, freckles; still in his school uniform.

'Aren't you too young to be smoking?'

'Ain't you too old to give a fuck?'

'Fair comment.'

He sat down and lit up.

'You got any money?'

I shook my head. I wasn't scared, why would I be? I honestly couldn't give a Shanghai shit.

'You've been smoking,' Susan sighed as she hung my coat in the hall cupboard, 'I can smell it on your scarf.'

'I had one. Some little tyke took the rest off me at knifepoint.'

No doubt the scarf would be the next thing to go to the church jumble; I contaminated it with the scent of a good time.

'Wash your hands,' she said. 'I've made you a sandwich.'

It didn't matter that I wasn't hungry; it was made. I waited until she went upstairs to run a bath and threw it in the bin. I hadn't felt hungry for some time, I'd tried to talk to Susan about it, but she didn't seem to want to know.

*　*　*

She was in the bath when I found out we'd won, not three or four numbers. The full six. I would tell her the next day. I'd go out and buy champagne and flowers and tell her over Sunday dinner. She loves white lilies and pink champagne.

Then it happened. I stopped feeling anything. One minute Dale Winton babbled on about his *big money balls*, the next nothing. The radio stayed on upstairs. Susan always liked to listen to the Saturday play in the bath. She'd be wondering where I was with her cup of tea.

I tried to stand up, but my body didn't want to. I lay there for ages, screaming. Why couldn't anyone hear me? Was she really so tuned out?

'Where's my cup of tea?' I heard her on her way down the stairs.

She was wearing a pair of pink slippers that her sister bought on Dudley market. Susan always sounded more relaxed after a bath, less ready for a fight.

'Did you forget?' she said.

And for a moment it was all normal, nothing different.

Then her voice changed.

'Alfred!' she cried and grabbed my wrist. Like she was trying to find a pulse. She gave up, threw down my arm, put her head on my chest, then next to my mouth.

I wanted to breathe out.

I wanted to tell her it was ok.

I wanted to tell her about the win.

But it was too late.

She collapsed on the floor and sobbed. What was this? From the woman who rationed affection like wartime butter in the war?

She held my hand and stroked my face, and for a single moment, the old Susan was back, but it was too late because the old Alfred was gone.

***

She sat for hours, talking and talking, like she'd been vaccinated with a gramophone needle. She said all the things I wanted her to say, things I thought she'd forgotten how to say. I know I'm as much to blame. We should never have married. We were both too selfish. It was hardly a match made in heaven.

Susan never struck me as the sort who'd want the coffin in the house and yet she sits here every evening, talking away.

Where do all these words come from?

Where were they when it mattered?

If only I could tell her about the ticket, give her something to make her happy.

Outside the blackbird goes about his business. Hops across the lawn and then into the tree and then into the sky, his song like laughter.

'I'm taking your coat to the jumble,' she says. 'Someone might as well get the benefit.'

The first brick

When the United Kingdom voted to leave the European Union, and the odious term 'Brexit' was coined, I wept. It hated how my freedom and the freedom of others was being taken away, without a thought for what this really meant. I found myself in a country I no longer recognised. A country conned into believing the past was still there, just hidden behind posters of Brussels. They voted for warm beer, cricket on the village green novelty of a black face, power cuts, walk-outs and poverty. And so I wrote this story.

It started with a single brick. Not the one that the smiling Lady Mayor now taps with a trowel as she poses for pictures.

Not one of us ever this is how it might end when it crashed through Anna's front window. Glass flew everywhere, and all she did was look embarrassed. She couldn't apologise enough as she fussed around us, picking up shards as her fingers bled.

We had to force her to sit.

'It's kids,' I said. 'And we can call the council to fix the damage.'

'Until next time,' she whispered.

'There won't be a next time.'

Anna's eyes became wide. 'That's what I said when they put dog shit through letter-box.'

I searched for support from the others. Both Narinder and Meg shook their heads. Out of their depth. I asked Anna why anybody would do this, and when she answered, her eyes refused to find mine.

'They want us to go away. Back to Poland.' She stood and brushed herself down. 'I will phone council. One of you will pick up Pyotr? I cannot leave flat. Take him to your house until later.'

Narinder volunteered.

And it sowed the seeds. I needed to do something. But at that exact moment, I didn't know what.

* * *

'Jonathan *is* very smart,' his form teacher said, and I wondered how many other eager parents had basked in disconnected praise. All I cared about was his place at Brighouse.

'Do you think he'll get in?' I said and her smile flickered.

'His creative writing is excellent. His stories are *so* clever. Where we might need to focus is…'

She paused strategically, as if to oblige me time to enjoy this rush of joy before she pulled out a pin to burst any bubble.

'We need to concentrate on his numbers.'

'He knows his times tables. I test him all the time.'

'He's the first with his hand up for *six times five*, but when it comes to applying himself…'

Thirty, is all I can think. *Six times five is thirty.*

'Can I put him down for extra classes?'

Miss Taylor's brow furrowed. 'We have been forced to bring in a nominal fee.'

'That's fine.'

'You don't want me to tell you how much?'

'I want him to get into Brighouse,' I said, and hoped this didn't make me sound like one of those helicopter mothers who hang around the park and bawl encouragement at bewildered kids. The sort who knock themselves out trying to buy the right end-of-term gift - or bribe - for the teachers.

Afterwards, as Jonathan threw himself around in the burger bar ball-pool,

THE FIRST BRICK

I picked at leftover fries and dared myself to find out what *nominal fee* meant.

My eyes watered.

***

Our *Mummy Club* meets every Wednesday. Anna, Meg, me and Narinder. We bring sandwiches and sit together in the shade of a tree while the kids get to run wild.

'Have any of you considered after-school classes?' I said as I handed around custard creams.

Anna shook her head. 'I cannot pay.'

Narinder agreed. 'We wanted to send Ranjit, but Sanjay thinks *I* should be able to teach him. Like I don't already have a full-time job keeping house and playing *the politician's wife*.'

That's our nickname for her. Sanjay stood as an independent in the last by-election against a hateful Tory who campaigned hard on immigration. The winds must have blown in strange directions because he won by 31 votes. It changed Narinder's life.

Meg has remained silent. I knew she fretted about Brighouse. We often split a bottle of wine and talked about the alternative: a school on the far side of town. Two bus rides away and hemmed in by high fences with airport-grade security. Last year, two kids ended up in hospital after a knife fight.

'I'm already up to my eyeballs paying for our Rebecca's City & Guilds in hairdressing,' she said. 'We can't afford the practice wigs. She's having to back-comb next door's Alsatian.'

'We should do something,' I said. 'Our kids deserve better.'

I lay awake that night and remembered when that brick sailed through Anna's window and into our lives. Until then, Brexit was something that everybody else cared about. It didn't touch us. We'd been sitting together eating napoleonka, when it landed on the table where the kids had been doing homework minutes earlier.

I wrapped myself around my husband. 'We need to build something new.'

His eyes slowly opened. 'Am I snoring, love? Roll me over.'

I kissed the back of his neck, and he fell back to sleep. My mind whirred. I knew what we could do. I couldn't wait to see the others.

It was Meg who poured the coldest water. 'I can't do anything. What use would I be?'

'You could auction your services as a childminder, and people are constantly putting cards in the post office for cleaners.'

'Is that all I'm good for? Tidying up other people's shit.'

'That's what we'd all be doing,' I said. 'Putting right the crap.'

Somehow my plan to make something out of nothing had turned into re-opening the community centre. Narinder would front the after-school classes to resurrect her teaching career. I'd do the books - like I used to for Mercian Windows before maternity leave morphed into redundancy. Lovely Anna would bake. And as the most organised of us, Meg would manage the place.

Together we'd fundraise.

'Head shaving,' Meg said, and her face lit up. 'We bought our Rebecca clippers. She could shave heads for money.'

'Brilliant, and I could do face painting.'

Our garage is piled high with a job lot of ever-so-slightly toxic face painting kits that Dave bought on eBay. He clicked the wrong button, and the seller refused a refund. They're perfectly safe if you wash them off after an hour.

Narinder suggested henna tattoos.

'I'll bake,' Anna said, and the deal was done. On Saturday, we'd have our first community day.

I talked Mike from the *Dog and Duck* into letting us use his car park and it went down a storm. We raised a fortune. Nothing like enough to build a new community centre, but it was a start.

The first brick in our wall.

The local paper sent along a geeky guy with yellow teeth, and he took a few pictures. Anna flirted and gave him extra apple pie. Meg teased her something rotten.

'He has kind eyes,' Anna protested.

'Quite a nice arse too.'

'Four local women come together to build their future,' he wrote, and we toasted each other with Nescafe Gold.

The second community day was an even bigger hit, and by the time we arranged the third, we needed something bigger than a pub car park.

Narinder nagged Sanjay who nagged the council into letting let us use the playing fields and thanks to Meg stalking a local radio phone-in, we got a mention and the crowds surged.

I was painting a kid to look like a toxic tiger when I heard Anna's raised voice.

'You *have* to pay.'

A gang of kids helped themselves to pastries and pies. Some ended up on the floor, others were thrown.

I called for support and everyone descended.

Have you ever seen those films the fire brigade put out to warn you how quickly flames can engulf a room if your curtains are flammable? It was like that. The chaos took hold fast. Raised voices, punches thrown. When my eyes next opened, our beautiful day was in ruins.

'It's me,' Anna sobbed after. 'They hate me. I am Polach who came here and stole from them.'

'Stole what?'

'That is problem,' she said, her breath ragged. 'I don't *know* what I took. If I did, they could have it back.'

The newspaper guy was there again, and he let her cry on his shoulder.

'I hate the people in this town,' Narinder said. 'They give no one a reason to help.'

'We can't give up,' I said, though everyone else looked less sure.

I added up the money from three community days. It couldn't be right?

'Dave,' I said. 'Imagine they asked you to quote to convert the garages near the park into flats or something, what would you reckon it might cost?'

He did that builder's whistle thing that drives me insane.

'Ballpark,' I said. 'It's not like I'll hold you to it.'

'It's a big job, love. You wouldn't see much change out of 100k.'

'That's what I thought.' I looked again at the figure on my computer screen. 'How about if you converted just one of them?'

'You'd still have to cover basics. But I dare say I could do it for under 40.'

'Right, and that's all done and dusted, walls plastered, electrics, lighting, the lot.'

'Basic finish, but yeah… I reckon.'

'When can you start?'

Anna sat out the next community day. She came along for an hour and helped me paint faces, but there was something in her eyes that told me her heart had left town.

It was after as we shared a cup of tea that she dropped the bombshell.

'I have agreed to take Pyotr to see his grandmother.'

'That'll be nice, love. I bet she's not seen him in years. They grow so fast at his age.'

She stared off into the distance.

'You have been such a good friend, Julie. I will always remember.'

A penny dropped.

'You're not coming back, are you?'

'They threw paint at front door yesterday. Red paint. Like blood, I suppose. It isn't safe for us here.'

I rallied the others and together we did our best to change her mind. To our faces she agreed, but two days later, Anna called from Poland.

'I had to go,' she said. 'You see that?'

And I suppose I did.

* * *

As the Lady Mayoress stepped down from the podium, her speech about bringing the community together delivered. I took her place.

'This building isn't only for us,' I said. 'It's for a woman who inspired me. It's for a woman who tried to be a part of everything around her, but was driven out.'

My voice faltered and next to me, Narinder took my hand. She was always the practical one. The voice of reason when mine got carried away.

'Read what Anna wrote,' she said.

THE FIRST BRICK

When I tried but failed, Meg nudged me to one side and took over.

'I wanted to be there with you today,' she read from Anna's email. 'I wanted to see the faces on our children when we told them what we have done, and how we made something out of nothing. I will never forget the friends I made. You will be in my heart forever.'

All three of us were a blubbering mess as we left the tiny platform, and I saw my Jonathan roll his eyes. Chances are he'll be ribbed something awful at school on Monday.

I took a glass of bubbly and painted on a smile for the geeky local news guy. When done, he put down his camera and shook my hand.

'I thank you,' he said. 'You helped us find each other.'

'I'm sorry I...'

He nodded, and I followed his gaze across the patch of mud that would soon be flower beds and my heart sang.

'Anna,' I cried, and pushed through the crowd to gather her in a hug.

'I *had* to be here,' she said, her own tears as big and wet as mine. 'You made me see it does no good to run away. And there was Ryan too.'

Geeky guy had his arm around her.

'You two?' I said. 'You're together?'

We danced until it grew dark, which is when the council insisted we needed to turn down the noise and go back inside.

* * *

Next week is another community day and another chance for the four of us to marshal everyone we know into building funds to convert the next garage. Narinder has bugged Sanjay into pulling strings, and he mentioned the project in an interview with *The Guardian*. We launched a *Kickstarter* page, and the money has rolled in.

People *are* good at heart. They only want to help.

Every apple box has a bad one, or whatever it is the Jackson Five sang.

The ones who threw paint, who broke up a party, who threw that first brick. This is their doing. They strengthened us.

Their brick built our walls.

Magnolia

I'm sick of magnolia. All my life, I've wanted yellow, purple, red and bright green.

My mother had magnolia walls at a time when decent people had flock. The neighbours used to talk about the woman who couldn't afford wallpaper and who left her curtains open and played piano in a nightdress.

It took me years to realise they meant her.

'Those golf clubs have to go,' I tell him. 'It's not like you use them. Claire reckons I'd get fifty quid on eBay. And before you say it, I know you paid three times that. They will only get in the way when I decorate.'

I married in magnolia. I wanted white, but Mum refused.

'You're three months gone,' she said. 'People will talk.'

He'd have been fifty-three next Tuesday.

'Claire helped me sort out some of your clothes for the charity shop,' I say. 'Half of those shirts haven't been worn. I don't know what possessed you to buy them.'

He says nothing. He sits there and lets me go on. But he'll have seen the pots of paint.

I love yellow.

I know it's not everyone's cup of tea, but on a day like today, when everything feels misty and miserable, it cheers me up.

* * *

'What do you think to that?' I say when I finish the walls. 'Bit of a bold move.'

I paint the doors purple. Raucous purple. And the skirting board gets a coat of red gloss. The brightest in the shop. I've not decided what to do with the green.

'Are you sure about this?' Claire said when I told her my plans. 'Isn't it too soon?'

'If I leave it any longer, they'll carry me out in a box with the walls still magnolia.'

'It's not like you though. When Dad died, you wouldn't let anyone touch a thing.'

'Maybe I've changed.'

Last night, I burnt the net curtains. Out in the garden. Right in the middle of his bloody prized lawn. The new woman next door popped her head over the fence.

'It's early for bonfire night,' she said. She's not local. I think her accent is Welsh.

I told her I was getting rid of stuff and she did that thing everyone always does. Her head cocked to one side, and she gave me a sad smile. It's supposed to convey support, I suppose.

'Is everything all right?' she said. 'Do you want me to ring someone?'

'Piss off,' I muttered under my breath. 'I'm not bloody senile.'

I don't even know her. She's only lived there five minutes. I saw in the paper she's after permission to build a conservatory. It'll block the light from my garden. Why Patrick and Nigel had to sell up, I'll never know. They were nice boys. They didn't have nets. Or magnolia.

'Everything's fine, thanks for asking,' I said, and she went back in. But I saw her watching me from an upstairs window. I could have waved, but I let her think I didn't notice.

The piano needs tuning. I've not played it for years.

'Actually,' I tell him. 'You're the only person who knows I *can* play.'

When it gets dark, I switch on the lights and it feels like being in the middle of a van Gogh painting. Like the one we saw when you took me to Amsterdam for our golden anniversary. Gaudy, you called it.

'Tell you what,' I say. 'Tomorrow we'll see colours.'

MAGNOLIA

* * *

I ring Claire, and she drives us to Clent Hills. She says she'd love to come up, but she needs to make a call. She loves her mobile phone.

'You don't mind, do you?' she says without looking up from the screen.

'Of course not.'

I was going to ask her to give us time alone, anyway.

I'm wearing my new coat. The one I bought for the funeral. Everyone said what a nice service it was. The vicar made it sound like he knew you. Funny little onion, all things considered. He came round and talked for hours about God having a plan for everyone.

'You've got it very nice in here,' he said. 'It's very calming. What do they call this colour again?'

'Magnolia,' I said sourly.

'Ah.' He closed his eyes and smiled. 'Magnolia dodecapetala.'

'I'm thinking of redecorating,' I said.

'You shouldn't make any big decisions or big changes for the first twelve months, Mrs Edwards. Don't move house, don't buy a new car and don't change your job.'

'I'm retired.'

He had the decency to blush.

It's slippery under foot. We've had a dreadful summer. Rained nearly every day. Didn't stop the water board banning hose-pipes.

When we reach our place, I sit.

'Just look at the colours,' I say. 'Autumn's my favourite season. Do you remember when we were courting? You used to bring me to this bench all the time.'

I swallow hard.

'I have to let you go now, Eddie. I hope I'm doing the right thing.'

Nobody tells you how to scatter ashes. I pour and hope they don't land in an undignified heap.

A breeze picks him up and carries him out over the hillside. Down the slope where we once rolled, laughing like kids. People used to stop and stare.

At our age, we should have known better.
    He mixes with leaves. The yellows, browns, purples and reds.
    And I wish I was with him.
    A part of the colours.
    No longer magnolia.

Dead man's shoes

'Dead man's shoes, that's what he's wearing, Amy.' Angela winked as she spoke. 'The poor sod won't know what hit him.'

Afterwards, she sat at her desk licking the chocolate off a digestive biscuit. It smudged around her mean lips and I wondered out loud how she slept at night.

'Very well, thank you,' she said. 'You can't let yourself get involved.'

'But aren't you the personnel manager?' I asked, and she pulled one of her angry faces.

'Human Resources,' she said. 'That's different.'

I wanted to ask how it might be different, but she clarified that conversations were over by turning away and tapping at her keyboard.

I wondered about my own shoes. Was I dead too?

A few days later we were in the kitchen making tea at about the same time. Angela breezed in, humming tunelessly.

'I've let you do the next one,' she said, and I knew at once what she meant.

'I'm not sure I'm ready.'

'Nonsense,' she said with a click of the tongue and a smile. 'It's only hard the first time, after that it becomes like clockwork. We're in Room Six.'

I had ten minutes to read up on Martin Schultz. He was 42, divorced with two kids. His crime was calling in sick twice in a three-month period. This took his department average above the acceptable level.

'Everyone gets ill,' I said, but Angela shook her head.

'Nobody is ever so poorly they can't struggle in.'

'But doesn't that mean passing it on to everyone else?'

'That's an old wives' tale.'

'But I did my thesis on *sick building syndrome*.'

'That makes you an old wife,' she said, and laughed at her own joke. The other girls in the office joined in. Though their laughter felt forced. Like they were doing their duty, like they knew I had lots to learn.

'Anyway,' she said, 'look at this.'

It's an invoice for home office furniture. The company has a policy of paying towards the set up of space for people to work from home. Take up is low and we send emails once a month. Schultz had made a claim.

'Indulgent,' Angela says with a sour note. 'I told him as much and he didn't look sorry.'

'But it's within limits.'

She shakes her head angrily. 'We don't need people like this.'

The paperwork was never ending. Forms to end his pension, his health insurance, his gym membership and Internet connection. Letters to send to his doctor, his dentists and bank manager. Our company prided itself on offering significant benefits, taking care of every aspect of an employee's life. When the end comes, they're cast adrift. We take away every agreeable thing. Angela compares it to the end of a relationship and she's right. The paperwork makes it feel like a nasty divorce with neither side willing to admit there was ever a time when they were in love.

With Schultz waiting in the next room, I completed online forms to tip off the tax office and warn them he'd been let go following unusually high sickness.

Did this person make themselves unemployed?

'Tick yes,' Angela said. 'If they check and we've not been honest, it's us who gets it in the neck. They send so much bloody paperwork.'

'He's got kids to look after. Won't this stop him getting benefits?'

'Daddy should have thought of that when he was lying in his bed while others did his job.'

'Don't we owe all staff a duty of care?'

'Dead man's shoes,' she said solemnly. Her answer every time.

Martin Schultz turned out to be a nice bloke who blushed when I shook his hand. He even tried to crack a joke with Angela as she acted like a stranger.

I had to ask the right questions, in the right order.

'Do you know our policy on absenteeism?'

He nodded, but Angela insisted he answer out loud.

'Why,' he blurted full of accusation. 'Are you recording this, will anything I say be used against me?'

'There's no need for that,' she mocked, unable to make eye contact.

'There's every need if you ask me.'

Angela tutted, shook her head sharply and scribbled something on her notepad. I've seen her do this before, it's a nasty trick designed to intimidate.

'What's that you wrote?' Martin said.

'A note for later.'

'Later? Are we having another meeting, then?'

Angela gave me a look and scrawled *TELL HIM!!!* on her notepad. But I couldn't. There were more boxes to tick, and three mandatory questions.

'Were you ill on the 14th?' I say. 'And the 22nd, and the 23rd?'

'I don't know. Possibly. I've been off twice. You can check on my time sheet. Everyone's coming down with the same bug. It's sick building syndrome.'

'Finally, do you have a note from your doctor for either occasion?'

Schultz shakes his head. 'Surely I don't need one for brief absences. At least that's what it says in the staff handbook.'

'You don't,' I say, and before I dig further holes, Angela steps in.

'So you've been reading the staff handbook, have you? That's interesting. Any reason?'

He shakes his head and looks to me for support. I'm about to speak when Angela takes over. 'It's time to re-examine our relationship, Mr Schultz.'

He laughs, but it's not a joyful sound. 'Our relationship?'

'Somewhere along the way, I feel we've lost you.'

He says nothing, instead choosing to stare at the table, his arms folded.

'Obviously, situations such as these happen all the time, and what matters is that neither side takes it as a fault. The last thing we want to do is talk blame.'

He holds up a hand to speak. 'Are you firing me?'

Angela sits back and smiles at me. It's my job to deliver the final blow.

'We're letting you go,' I say meekly.

His eyes grow wide. 'After eight years? This will cost you.'

'If you check your contract, you'll see...'

'If *you* check your conscience, *you'll* see...'

Angela leans in close as if she's in the room to make sure we all play nice. 'I realise this is an emotional time for everyone. You've been with us for some years and it's never easy to end a relationship.'

'We don't have a *relationship*,' he says reasonably. 'I work here. That's all.'

Angela pulls a sheet of paper from a buff folder, slides it across the table and stands. 'This meeting is over. You need to read this letter and sign to show acceptance.'

Afterwards she takes me into a side room and complains how I handled things badly. 'You needed to stay on message. Don't let him cause you to deviate.'

'But *you* interrupted. You wrote something down, and it wound him up.'

She chuckles to herself. 'People need to grow thicker skins. Sick bloody building syndrome.'

* * *

One girl in HR told me Angela has a miserable life, and they reckon that's why she's like she is. Her husband's in a wheelchair and her mother's gone doo-lally. Last they heard she was in next door's garden taking in the washing. Angela's had special locks fitted to keep her mother from going outside when there's nobody looking.

'Isn't that like keeping someone in prison?' I say.

Maybe it's the stress that has caused Angela to smoke again.

'You'll never guess what I heard about William Barlow.' Her voice rattles during a departmental meeting. 'Apparently he's into kinky stuff. He wears those leather trousers with the bum cut out.'

'Chaps,' I say, without thinking.

She looks at me curiously. 'Is that what they're called? Well anyway, he had them delivered from a mucky bookshop in London.'

'Did the parcel get ripped?'

'No, I opened them,' she says. 'It was a suspicious-looking package. I had to check for security reasons.'

The others grin, like this is a nugget of information to store and use.

'It's like thingy in the finance team,' someone else says. 'She had a vibrator delivered.'

The others laugh like drains, but I don't want to know stuff like this. I'll not be able to look at *thingy in finance* or William Barlow without thinking they know that I know.

'Billy Boy likes other men to wee on him.' Angela is back on her subject. 'I read it in an email.'

'You can't do that,' I say, scandalised.

'Check the HR policy,' she says. 'Company systems should only be used for company purposes. When I saw he was having personal items delivered, I followed my instincts and did a bit of detective work. He's coming to see us after lunch. You can handle this one on your own Amy. I've prepared all the paperwork.'

'You're firing him?'

'Unreasonable behaviour. The dirty little tyke. Having men wee over him and then coming in here.' She shudders. 'Touching things.'

'That's not how it is.'

'And how would you know?'

'It's none of our business what he does in his own time.'

'No,' Angela says sharply. 'But it *is* our business when he uses company email to arrange his sex life.'

She laughs, but it causes her to cough, splutter and choke. Her face turns purple and her jowls shake.

* * *

One morning, Angela didn't come in, and it surprised everyone. Off ill, for the first time in fifteen years.

'What's wrong,' I said. 'Did she bite her own tongue and have to find someone to suck out the poison?'

The girls in HR went quiet and exchanged looks.

'It's a joke,' I said, but none of them smiled.

She was off again the next day and the next. And then, word came she'd collapsed and her neighbours had called an ambulance. An envelope did the rounds, collecting money for flowers and a card. I must have been one of the first to get it because the collection was almost empty.

They put Audrey from Finance in charge. Angela would be furious. She detests Audrey and calls her *fur coat, no knickers*.

Martin Schultz emailed to ask who to quote as a reference. He'd found another job and wanted to know he could count on someone to remember better times. I went to see his manager, an American guy called Rick.

'Gee,' he said. 'I'm not sure. I *guess* he was a great guy and all, but if I say the wrong thing, won't we get into all kinds of legal stuff? I had an email from Angela right after you fired him.'

'This is his life,' I say, not unreasonably, and Rick promises to sleep on it.

Knowing Rick has no spine, I write the reference and send it off.

Audrey introduces flexible working. Word reaches Angela, and she struggles back in. There's a meeting arranged, and an email follows. Angela is taking early retirement.

There's another collection and a much bigger card. Once more, very little money reaches the envelope. It does two rounds of the office.

* * *

When we hear of her passing, there's a strange air of shock. She was ill, of course, but we all thought not *that* serious. Angela never seemed the sort to die. We all expected her to rise again like Lazarus and make more lives miserable. A whisper suggests she hid how sick she was for years.

When her collection barely makes double figures, the company chips in to send flowers and arrange a send off. Not quite a wake, more like *after-work drinks* in a nearby bar with salmon paste sandwiches. Interest stays low, and the invite gets extended to former staff.

I run into Martin Schultz at the bar, and he looks so much younger. I ask how he's keeping, and he smiles. 'Better now. It was rough for a while, but that reference you wrote helped.'

'That came from Rick.'

He glances over to where Rick hangs with his team and does his level best to avoid eye contact. 'We both know that's not true.'

Martin gets me a drink, and we merge with the crowd.

'What made you come tonight?' I say. 'It's not like things ended well.'

He snorts. 'I suppose I wanted to be sure the witch was truly dead.'

'Am I imagining it, but you two used to be friends?'

He nods. 'Angela turns like the wind, Amy. I'm not sure exactly what I did to upset her.'

I tell him about the home furnishing emails and he looks shocked. 'Did she think that mattered enough to try ruining me?'

Martin puts his drink down and collects his coat. 'I think it's best I go.'

'You should stay awhile,' I say. 'You have friends here.'

Martin shakes his head. 'This is a celebration for the life of a woman who only ever saw the bad in people. I need to breathe better air.'

As the evening draws to a hanger-on close, I sit next to Audrey. Now fully in charge and determined to make things better.

'Did *you* learn anything from Angela?' she says. 'Truthfully?'

I think for a moment. 'Only how not to treat others.'

She nods and smiles to herself. 'Dead man's shoes?'

Berlin, baby

There's a reason Berlin hotels offer attractive room rates in January. Nobody wants to go. It's cold. Colder than anywhere you've ever been. Think about how cold that is, then imagine it colder.

Did that stop me and my beloved from booking a fancy schmanzy hotel and first class travel to the once divided German capital? 'We'll wrap up warm,' I said. Prices like this are too good to miss.

On a Friday morning at the start of February, we boarded the aptly named ICE train at Amsterdam Centraal. Fellow passengers wore fur-lined coats, hats and Cossack boots. It was the first hint we might have it wrong.

Six hours later, Berlin's Hauptbahnhof loomed. Thrilled by iconic architecture, we charged from heated indoors into crisp open air. Iconic buildings everywhere. OK, it was a tad chilly – bone-numbingly cold, perhaps. But what the heck, we'd get a nice warm taxi to our nice warm hotel then find a nice warm bar for dinner and a few beers.

But back to the main point of this. I can't stress it enough. It was cold.

On our first evening, we searched for somewhere, anywhere to eat and walked miles. 'Please can we go in somewhere,' I whined, as all feeling below the waist vanished. Eventually, we did what all good culture vultures do when in Germany. We ate Greek. I fought back the start of a sniffle.

Our cunning plan to beat over-enthusiastic central heating by opening a window left our room feeling like a fridge.

'Ah ha,' says I. 'This is a job for a steaming hot bath.'

Submerged in the gloriously warm water, limbs regained feeling. This was when I noticed the bathroom floor was two inches under water–as was our room. I heard the fizz of a travel iron as the lights went out. Not only in our room, it turned out, judging by the subsequent angry hammering on our door.

In a move that felt like punishment, the barely smiling Fräulein on reception handed over keys to a room that had all the charm of a wrestler's spittoon.

'It's the only room left,' she said when I went back to complain. Fair enough, I thought, we'll manage. She had good cause to be miffed in the face of a queue of disgruntled guests. Guests who found themselves without water or electricity.

She said something in German I took to mean, 'That is the stupid English bastard who caused all this trouble.'

The next morning at breakfast, conversation stopped as we walked in. People nudged each other in the hotel foyer. Out and about, I'm certain fingers were pointed.

I swear a woman in the KaDeWe told her friend, 'That's the pair who fused half the lights in the city.'

And it was still cold.

By Sunday morning, a sniffle gave way to flu. Not man flu. The real thing–throwing up, shivering, aching all over, unable to get out of bed flu.

'Rooms must be vacated by ten,' insisted reception. The implication being that the hotel pet Alsatians wanted their room back.

The train journey back was miserable. The carriage sounded like a mobile chest clinic, with fellow travellers coughing and wheezing and groaning into Amsterdam, where I took to my bed and vowed to never again book anything that seemed too good to miss.

First published in The Observer, February 2007

The vicious queen

Ryan hates his job. He hates the tram that takes him into the centre of Amsterdam. He hates the way his access pass hardly ever works, leaving him hammering on a heavy oak door. Above all of this, he hates his boss.

Everyone else *loves* Ryan's boss. They think he's camp and funny and such brilliant company.

'Greg's great at talking to people,' they all say. 'He makes everyone laugh.'

Ryan stops himself short of saying how much better it would be if Greg ever listened to anything anyone said. He never listened when Ryan told him he wasn't gay, but if he were, he'd be flattered. Twice.

When his machine wakes, Ryan checks email. Sixteen today from Greg. Each one asking for something ASAP. They come with little red flags to confirm the urgency and as he clicks, unseen messages fire off to confirm receipt.

Greg ends every message with a smiley face.

'Morning!'

Ryan looks up to see Marianne take off her coat.

'It's so cold today,' she says and rubs her arms as if this will make a difference. The office heat is up full, it's like a sauna.

'How can you sit there with no sweater?' she says, and she makes it sound like the most awful character flaw. Her sing-song accent makes her sound like a little girl, unbecoming for a 40-year-old mother of two.

He wants to tell her it's not that cold, instead he nods. 'Where did the sun go, eh?'

'It's in the sky, silly.' Marianne wrinkles her nose and laughs at her own joke.

It will be *one of those days*. How long until someone halfway normal gets in? Half-past-eight. At least another hour.

His Inbox pings. Yet another mail from Greg. He could answer it now or get coffee.

'I'm making a drink,' Ryan says. 'You want one?'

Marianne makes a face like he's offering a dose of poison. 'It's so bad for you. You should drink water.'

'That's what I used to make the coffee.'

'Ach, no, it's not what I mean.'

Marianne folds her arms, and unless Ryan makes a dash for it, he'll get another lecture on the evils of caffeine.

'I'll take that as a no,' he says and dives for the door.

In the kitchen, one of the elderly women employed to keep the place clean runs a filthy floor cloth across a marble worktop. She stinks of fags and rose water.

'Morning Ilse,' he says and although she doesn't answer, he knows she's heard.

Agnes, the head of HR comes in, takes a mug from the cupboard and fills it with scalding water. She rattles away in Dutch, even though there's a company rule that declares English to be the working language. When three or more *associates* (that's what they call staff) gather in the same room they should *always* speak English. Out of respect for each other.

Agnes wrote that rule. She breaks it every day.

'How are you?' Ryan says, determined to force his way in.

Agnes sighs, turns slowly around and looks him up and down. 'Fine.'

And then she switches back to Dutch.

It wasn't always like this. Agnes took a real shine to Ryan when he started six years ago. They were early morning people and in the days when they both smoked she used to shower him with company secrets. They both kicked the habit, but the gossip continued. Early morning heart-to-hearts. Stuff about which he couldn't care less, but because she seemed to need someone to talk to, he listened.

Her mother was ill. Her partner was a drain. She hated living in the sticks. Did I hear about Sonia from the management team? She lost the baby. Hardly surprising given how much she liked a drink.

Then Agnes decided she didn't like him.

Ryan didn't much care; it was less to listen to.

Tania walks in. She's six-foot-three, skinny as a beanpole and everyone's friend. Agnes once told him how much Tania earns. Twice his own salary. 'Did you read that email from Greg?' she says before she's even sat down.

'Which one?'

'The one about the website. He said something about it not working on his mobile.'

Ryan *had* seen it. Sent it at 2am. Greg had texted too, just to make sure. It had woken him. 'I'll look.'

'He said it was kind of urgent.'

'It always is.'

Tania tries for a smile, but he knows she's itching to go into another room to ring Greg and report insubordination.

'I'll get to it right away,' Ryan said, and she looked disappointed.

Two people call in sick. Claire and Neil. The sane ones. John, his team leader, rolls in at six minutes past ten. The rule is everyone must be at their desk and ready to work by ten. It's John's rule. 'I got stuck talking to Francis,' he says.

Nobody looks up. He gets stuck talking to someone most days.

By lunchtime, all of Greg's messages are answered. Not one of them felt remotely urgent.

John emails to ask if Ryan can spare time for a chat. He looks up. Is this for real? They sit two desks apart, but his boss likes 'paper trails' and keeps *every* email.

Might as well play the game. He fires back a message to ask what this chat might be about. There won't be a reply.

Ryan makes a second coffee, inadvertently gate-crashing a birthday celebration. The IT team gathers round the long kitchen table, making small talk and balancing slices of cake on paper plates.

'Congratulations,' he says and shakes the hand of the birthday boy, hanging around to join in a chorus of *"Lang zal hij leven"*.

'You're not in this team,' says Brian, the sour-faced department manager. 'You didn't have cake, did you?'

Ryan shakes his head. 'I was getting coffee.'

Brian's lips purse. He wants to say something, but there's no crime committed. It'll get back to Greg, for sure. The news he sloped off work and joined a birthday celebration uninvited.

Brian and Greg think their relationship is a secret. It isn't.

'Where have you been?' John says when Ryan gets back to his desk. 'We need the project plan for support.'

'It's right here.'

Ryan picks up a folder across which he's scribbled the words *"Support Project Plan"*.

'You need to stay on top of these things,' John snaps.

'I was getting coffee.'

John takes the folder back to his desk, but doesn't open it.

Ryan feels so tired. It's been months since he slept the night through. He constantly wakes at 3am full of the terrors. Or an hour earlier when Greg texts orders. He lies still and watches Gill sleep, envying her lack of fear. He hates the fear even more than he hates John and Greg. Because he doesn't really know what there is to fear. Their rent is almost nothing. They go on holiday twice a year. Usually. Not last year, admittedly. John cancelled Ryan's holiday with a week's notice because Greg needed his online bio updated.

Ryan's jaw aches from grinding his teeth.

John sends another email mid afternoon. Ryan sees it pop up, but pretends not to notice. He knows it will drive his boss mad.

And then, miracles of miracles, John gets up from his desk and walks over.

'When are we having this chat?'

'What is this about?'

'Let's do this now. Agnes says we can use her office.'

Ryan's Inbox pings with another email from Greg. There's a capital letter missing from a headline on an obscure webpage. It needs to be corrected ASAP.

Red flag, smiley face, read receipt sent.

John is already hovering by the office door. ASAP will have to wait.

* * *

Agnes has an office that overlooks the air conditioning system. It means the window needs to stay shut and so the tiny room smells of Camel Lights and white linen. She's covered one wall with photos of nights out with former staff. People she used to gossip with Ryan about.

The two men sit either side of a small round table piled high with confidential salary slips. Ryan is shocked to see Diana in Finance earn so little.

John opens a folder filled with email printouts. 'Let's talk about how things have been going lately. I'm a little concerned you're not happy.'

'I'm fine.' Ryan hears his voice grow high-pitched, anxious even.

'You don't seem yourself.'

'What makes you say that?'

John picks up on the fact that Ryan has been trying to read the first e-mail upside down and closes the folder. It was from Agnes.

'Greg tells me you're struggling to keep up.'

'I'm sorry?'

'Greg reports he often has to wait a long while to get answers from you.'

'I always deal with everything as soon as I get it.'

John's mobile rings.

'One minute,' he says. 'This is Greg now.'

He leaves Ryan alone with the salary slips. He sees Greg's name, but something obscures the figures. If he moves it ever-so-slightly… Christ alive! That's obscene!

John's back. His face purple with rage. 'Greg says he sent you an email before lunch.'

'Probably.'

'We need to check now.'

Ryan follows John back to the office. At his desk he types in his password and flinches at the sight of unread emails, all from Greg. Some dated weeks earlier. Messages never seen before.

'I deal with *everything*,' he says. 'I don't know how…'

'We need to speak to Agnes,' John says. 'You best bring your bag and coat. I will need your security pass.'

'It doesn't work.'

'Did you report that?'

'No.'

John shakes his head and snatches the pass from Ryan's desk. 'Follow me.'

* * *

Ryan Walker wakes from a full night's sleep and looks across at Gill. Outside, he hears birdsong. Was it always there? She reaches across to stroke his cheek.

'We'll manage,' she says and for once, the words ring true.

September

'What if one of us dies?' he asks. It's another conversation about upping sticks and leaving the city.

'How is it any different to what we have here?' I say and he nods.

I sense the sadness.

You've done this, he wants to say. *You. Not me.*

Once, I'd have been overjoyed to live amongst noise, mess and people. Now I crave silence.

So we book a holiday. To the middle of nowhere to see if we like it. It's September 1st and the kids are back behind school gates. The beaches are empty. The forests deserted.

'I wish we could stay here,' he'll say, and we'll talk about how one day we'll live in a big house in an enormous field with chickens and dogs and a donkey. And I'll hurt when I sense I can't give him that.

Because I don't do off-grid life.

As I plod past 50, I do comfort and familiarity. I like predictable.

When I was thirty, I wore torn jeans and sold books and CDs to fund nights out. I went overdrawn or maxed-out credit cards.

Now I have a gold card.

A week in rural France no longer calls for a tent. It involves a converted barn with a dishwasher and microwave oven.

'What if we're living in the middle of nowhere and one of us dies?' he asks again.

'Let's open another bottle of wine,' I suggest and leave his question hanging, hating that uncertainty hurts him the most.

SEPTEMBER

People grow old. What once seemed fun becomes an anathema. So *what if* one of us dies? I think.

First published as part of the 3six5 Project; short pieces from 365 writers published over 365 days in 2010

Coming Home

Why do they sit around my bed and wait? Do they think I'm about to do tricks? They reckon I can't see them, although I think they've cottoned on to the fact I can hear.

Some bright spark plays songs by Daniel O'Donnell. And yesterday I forgot myself and squeezed someone's hand. I only wanted it to stop.

His voice drives me mad.

So now they talk at me rather than over me, doing the voice usually reserved for foreigners. Loud and slow. Pausing after each boring fact to see if I react.

I'm not going to. Sod them.

Yesterday Jennifer told Peter off for eating my grapes.

I'm not going to eat them, am I?

Why let them go to waste?

She was whispering, so I know she was trying to make sure I didn't hear. The thing is, I've discovered it is true what they say about how when one sense goes, the others grow stronger.

Ever since I shut my eyes, stopped tasting things, stopped touching things, every little sound got louder.

The nurse dropped a metal tray, and it was deafening.

I wanted to sit up and tell her to take more care, but I can't.

Nobody knows I've worked out how to force my eyelids open enough to see what's going on. It's blurred around the edges and I'm stuck with the one angle, but I've counted the faces.

Ben looks so upset, poor little mite. I don't know why they've brought him. It isn't the place for little ones.

COMING HOME

***

It was Thursday night when I took ill. I'd been feeling queer all day and when Joan came round to collect money for the papers I had a dizzy spell.

'Sit down pet,' she said, 'You look pale, have you been overdoing things?'

'I think I'm coming down with that cold that's going around,' I said. 'Doug from across the road said Pauline's been in bed with it since Saturday.'

'It's not bird flu is it?'

'I shouldn't think so. You know what Pauline's like. She's the sort who thinks she's having a heart attack if she so much as passes wind.'

'All the same, you need to take things easier.'

Joan made me a cup of tea and I drank it while we caught up.

I've not been going out much lately what with the bad weather and since my fall, I've been more careful.

The Internet is a wonderful thing though, I've been able to get my shopping delivered, so it's not as if I've gone hungry.

I told Joan about it.

'It's times like this you miss having a man around, isn't it?' she said and I smiled politely.

The last thing I missed was Sid. If it hadn't been for him and what he did to our Robert, I wouldn't be on my own now. The day he finally popped his clogs, I breathed a sigh of relief.

He was always a handful, our Robert.

Used to answer back and I was temped to give him a backhander on more than one occasion.

Even now I remember that night Sid lost his temper after he wouldn't take his hands out of his pockets and chucked a chair against the wall. The one time, Sid came home drunk after the football. It was the first and only time he hit me.

I carried on making sure his tea was on the table. I kept cleaning the house and every Friday night we sat together in the Dog and Duck.

He never laid another finger on me.

Even when he'd had a few drinks and tried to get fruity.

I'd push him away, and he'd roll over and go to sleep.

* * *

I danced on his grave the day they buried him. Literally. I waited until everyone had gone to eat cucumber sandwiches at the Labour Club and lifted my skirt, kicked up the soil and took your beautiful white roses and put them in a vase on our Robert's headstone.

Someone has hold of my hand.

It's Maureen.

How many times have I told her to blow not sniff?

I can't listen any longer.

It's all the same stuff about how they love me and how they'll miss me and why can't I stay longer?

I've somewhere else to be, Maureen.

I peep out one more time and see him there. At the back of the room, sitting in his chair, laughing.

'Mam?' he says and reaches out a hand.

Oh, how I've missed him.

How good it feels to come home.

Girl 32, considered attractive

'What are you doing with your tits?'

The voice is husky and whispered. An echo and the sound of water tells me this call comes from a bathroom. I picture pink pedestal mats and frosted glass as I lie about how I'm playing with my nipples, twisting and teasing, watching them grow hard under his tongue.

They're always more interested in what you're doing with your tits than what you look like. I've never once been asked to describe myself. They've already decided when they pick up the phone.

I bet his wife's downstairs. Making dinner. Pork chops, potatoes and peas. Should I feel sorry?

Thump, thump, thump.

I glance at the ceiling. My mother is on the move. 'Countdown' must have finished, so it's time for her evening meal. That's what she calls it. 'Her evening meal.' Not in tribute to my great kitchen skills. More to take the piss.

The pathetic grunts continue down the phone and I whisper I'm moist. That's one of their favourite words.

'Oh baby,' he breathes. 'Are you nearly there?'

I match him groan for moan and wait for the silence.

'Thank you,' a meek voice says. 'Thank you very much.'

He hangs up before I can say 'Please come again.'

It's one of my little jokes. Something to keep me smiling. Something to keep me in charge.

I fill a saucepan from the kettle. Soft-boiled eggs with bread and butter soldiers. It's Tuesday.

***

'You can't leave me on my own, what if I have a fall?' Mum peers over her glasses.

'You don't get out of bed. How are you going to fall?'

She puts down her spoon.

'I think I'd rather have scrambled eggs from now on.'

I take the plate and with the edge of a tea towel, dab a stream of yolk from her chin.

'We must change that nightie, Mum.'

On autopilot, I read from the local paper. She listens and nods.

'Read the obituaries,' she says after a while and I do.

Money's tight this month even with her allowances. I could have done without that letter about a school trip. I'm going to have to beg for extra shifts. Except not tonight. I can't. I already made plans.

It's as if Mum reads my mind.

'You're not going out tonight, are you, Susan?' she says.

'Harry's downstairs. He'll listen out for you.'

'You'll have the police round. They'll take him off you. You can't leave a six-year-old on his own in the house.'

'Harry's eleven,' I say. 'And anyway, Maureen from next door always keeps an ear out. If you need anything, thump the floor. I've put your stick where you can reach it.'

I hate the way her eyes reveal what she thinks of me.

'Make sure you're back in time to take my teeth out,' she says. 'I don't want strangers messing in my mouth.'

I kiss her forehead and brush what's left of her hair.

'Try to get some sleep.'

'Sleep's all I do these days,' she says. 'Tell your father to hurry up with the Horlicks. I don't want to miss "Book at Bedtime". '

Her eyes close.

***

'I need you to you look after Nan,' I tell Harry. 'I have to work.'

'Dressed like that?'

'It's an interview for a new job,' I lie. 'If I get it, then maybe I won't have to work so many hours.'

'You said you'd help with my geography project.'

I reach down my jacket. 'Tomorrow,' I say. 'I double promise.'

My mobile rings, another call from BabeLine. I thought I'd logged out. If I reject this one, they'll put me at the back of the queue when I next log on.

'Are you going to answer that?' he says.

'Make sure your Nan's OK,' I say. 'It's your Auntie Val. Read to her. She likes it when you do that.'

***

Fifteen minutes and one subservient Scot later, I'm on the bus across town and that's when the butterflies start.

I'm Girl 32, Considered Attractive. Good Sense of Humour. No ties.

In his advert, Ken claimed to be rugged but handsome, a sports fan who plays football on a Sunday. Like me, he didn't post a picture, but I know he's five foot eleven, with brown eyes and dark-brown, short cropped hair. He'll have a bunch of red roses. Bit naff. His suggestion.

God, but I'm nervous. This was Val's idea. I should never have listened.

'How else are you going to meet anyone?' she said. 'Stuck in all night with your mother. Up cleaning toilets at the crack of dawn.'

I reach my stop half an hour early.

Ken said 7.30.

I can't face the pub on my own, and so walk around the block.

A group of lads in hoodies gathers at the far end of the street, so I head in the opposite direction. Down to the church where we buried Dad.

It's locked up, so I follow a path round the back and into the graveyard. I've not been here for years. I used to come twice a week, extra at Christmas. Until Mum told me what he'd done.

I suppose I'd always known.

Everything is so overgrown. Neglected. Forgotten.

"Loving husband and father," it says on his grave.

The biggest joke going.

With time to kill, I pull out my phone and log back into BabeLine. Within seconds a call comes through.

'Is this Alisha?'

I lay back on Dad's grave, enjoying the feel of cool evening grass. There's still warmth in the sun and I close my eyes.

We do the whole tits, nipples and wet bush thing.

'I want to fuck you now,' he says and instinct parts my legs. My hand moves aside clean white knickers and I match him groan for moan, being outdoors lets me play the part to the full and I scream and I howl.

When he hangs up, I'm exhausted and lie so still to take pleasure in the breeze on my half naked body.

I look at my watch.

Shit! Ken will think I've stood him up.

I send a text to say I'm running late.

'Enjoy the show?' I say to Dad's stone. 'Remind you of the good old days?'

* * *

Ken turns out to be nice. He buys me drinks and the roses number twelve. He suggests we meet up again for supper. The word makes me shudder. If he'd only said dinner.

'We're not all bastards,' he says as he signs the credit card slip.

'I know.'

I allow myself to smile.

'So, Girl 32. What do you say to doing something at the weekend?'

'Ring me,' I say. 'We'll sort something.'

We kiss goodnight and I know I'll never see him again.

Not because I don't want to.

* * *

There's an ambulance outside when I round the corner. Flashing lights reveal familiar faces. Harry. Maureen from next door. Bob from across the way.

Two men wheel out a stretcher.

I try to run but things move in slow motion.

Harry calls out and runs over to throw his arms around me and buries his face, sobbing.

'What happened?' I ask. 'What went wrong?'

Maureen puts her arms around both of us.

'Sue, I'm so sorry,' she says. 'They want to know if you're going in the ambulance.'

'Did she fall?'

'She's unconscious. They say she's broken bones. The police are here. They want to have a word.'

While Mum sleeps, I answer questions in a side room. Did I think it was right to leave an eleven-year-old boy alone? Do I do this often? Is there a history of abuse in the family?

'He wasn't on his own. He was with my mother.'

I'm given a case number and warned there will be *follow up*. The doctor comes in to have a word. Mum's broken her collarbone and needs to stay in for a few days.

'How are things at home?' he says 'How are you coping?'

'Barely,' I admit.

They take Harry away to get a can of coke.

'No crisps,' I call after him. 'Not between meals.'

The doctor makes notes and says he must write a report for social services.

'How did it all happen?' I hear myself say.

'Your mother's very groggy,' he says. 'She said something about your father.' He looks up from his clipboard. 'Is he still alive?'

I shake my head. 'Not any more.'

* * *

Harry's doing his homework, sat up at the table when my mobile dances across the kitchen counter. I glance at the clock. Where did the last hour go?

'You going to answer that?' he says and I shake my head. 'Might be important.'

'It's probably someone trying to sell me double glazing.'

He looks anxious so I grab it and hit reply.

'What are you doing with your tits?'

'Wrong number,' I say and hang up.

Escape

He'd been sitting outside, on a bench. Hardly grounds to think him strange, but December 12th was the coldest of days. Snow lay thick and winds whistled round Victoria coach station. He wasn't dressed for such an awful day. His coat was thin and his trousers more suited to a walk on the beach. The colours he chose suggested summer and not deepest, darkest winter. Everyone around wore grey and blue, and he stood out in yellow and red.

Outside was where smokers lingered, and he wasn't one. Or if he was, he wasn't smoking now, and hadn't for the last fifteen minutes. Instead, he read a newspaper. The Guardian, but not today's edition. The photo on the front was of crying children, fleeing homes torn asunder by a tropical storm. Yesterday's news.

Now and then he'd glance around. His eyes darted from side to side, searching; as if waiting for a familiar face. You couldn't call his manner jumpy or agitated. Apart from the clothes, everything about him was so normal.

And then he stood up, shook himself, and left the newspaper behind.

I watched him traipse across the bus yard.

With distance, the colours he wore became more obvious. He didn't blend in. The sore-thumbness of a yellow jacket made him impossible to lose.

Two women wrapped in fake fur coats nudged each other and pointed.

How rude, I thought. How rude that they found him too different to ignore.

He bought coffee from a kiosk and spent forever stirring in sugar and fastening the plastic lid back in place. He spoke for a while to someone in uniform before heading back.

His eyes met mine and made me feel he'd known I was watching all along. I shifted my bag to let him sit, and conversation seemed unavoidable.

'All buses are cancelled,' he said. 'We're in for a long wait.'

Being trapped so far from home should fill me with fear, instead it left me intrigued. This was a man I wanted to understand.

'I know a place nearby,' he said. 'We could get something to eat. If the snow gets worse, they have rooms.'

We braved driving winds and wet snow. Men in long coats and women with umbrellas got in the way.

'Is it much further?' I said, and he waved to cross the road.

'It's just here.'

We stood in front of what looked like someone's house. There were no lights inside and he pulled a key from his pocket.

'Sorry,' I said. 'I thought this was a bar.'

'It's a private member's club. It's well disguised.'

He led the way through three sets of doors and into a hallway. From behind the door, I heard music and conversation.

'You can hang up your jacket,' he said.

Double doors opened, and I recognised the voice of the woman singing.

'Is that Kate Bush?'

A small crowd had formed around a piano. The woman playing was tiny but familiar. Older now and no longer prone to leotards. She wore black and looked magnificent. As she sang, her eyes closed.

'Where are we?' I said, and my friend took hold of my hand.

Someone had laid the table with silver and gold. Huge white plates and cloth napkins. I sat and soon the people from before came too. Kate sat beside me, but I was too shy to talk.

'You seem nervous,' she said. 'There's really no need.'

'I'm a huge fan,' was all I could manage.

She giggled. 'I rather thought you might be.'

My friend was back to tell me it was time to move on.

'But I haven't eaten.'

He insisted we were not here for dinner, and I peered past to where a woman held my coat.

The frost-fingered garden seemed to go on forever. As we walked through drifting snow, the air grew silent, light faded and when I next turned around, I was lost.

'Where are we?' I said, but there came no reply.

'Is this a dream? Have I fallen asleep in the coach station?'

Still, we walked on. Through a window, I gazed in on what looked like a party.

'That's my father,' I said, puzzled. 'How can he be here?'

He danced with a woman, elegant in black. She had long white hair and her eyes never left his.

'Who is she?' I asked.

'You don't recognise her?'

'No.'

'Look more closely.'

The eyes gave things away. And then the hands.

How well I looked.

'Am I dead?'

He laughed. 'You escaped.'

When my alarm clock sounded, I swiped for it. How could I be so dumb? It was half nine, my bus was due to leave at ten. I called home, and every excuse fell on deaf ears.

'I'll re-book,' I said into miffed silence. 'I'm so sorry.'

The coach company phone lines were busy. I looked through the window. Snow had fallen. In this country, it only takes a stray leaf on a railway track to bring chaos. Snow wreaks havoc. Suddenly the line went dead and when I tried again, there was nothing. I turned on my computer, but the Internet was slow.

Twitter, I thought. *I'll tweet about how shite the service is at National Express.*

When the page wouldn't load, I idly flicked to the news, expecting nothing but stories about snow.

Six gunmen and four suicide bombers struck in central London on December 12th, killing 106 people and injuring over 900. The co-ordinated attacks came on Victoria Coach Station as the morning rush hour drew to a close. Three bombs went off at or around 0850 BST just outside the waiting room, and a fourth on an incoming coach. Gunmen stormed the waiting rooms, mowing down passengers.

The lights are on

I came home and found my mother making pastry in her nightdress.

'Mum,' I said. 'What's wrong?'

But she didn't seem to hear, and it was only when I touched her arm that she stopped and landed a kiss on the end of my nose.

'He's left me,' she said in a matter-of-fact voice.

'Who has?'

'Your father.'

She headed for the pantry, leaving one slipper behind.

'Dad isn't with us any longer,' I said, as gently as I could manage.

She turned around, her arms full of jars and shrugged.

'Robert. You studied at University. Surely you understand what I said. Your father has left me. We're getting a divorce.'

The other slipper worked itself free of her foot, causing her to trip. There was a flash of red as raspberry jam hit the kitchen floor.

* * *

'This woman had shock,' said our Polish GP. 'She must get rest and take tablets.'

He reached into his briefcase to pull out a pad and pen and then took off his thick-rimmed glasses to scribble a prescription.

'Will Diana need to go to hospital?' Pam said, and the doctor stopped writing.

'Why would she need hospital?'

'She had a nasty fall.'

'Is just bruises. Ridiculous to waste hospital time. Rest and take tablets.'

'What sort of tablets?' I said, and he looked me up and down.

'Anti-depressant,' he said and handed Pam a slip of paper. 'You take to chemist. Take now and give one tonight with food. Never on empty stomach. Will not work at once, will take three months, then you notice big change.'

He stood to go.

'Anti-depressants,' I said carefully. 'You're aware of…'

He nodded sharply.

'I can read. The Polish education system is excellent.'

And with that he shook my hand.

Pam came to sit with me in the living room and for a while we didn't speak. We stared through the patio windows into Mum's overgrown back garden.

'Should we get these tablets?' I said more to myself than her.

'He *is* a doctor.'

'This morning she told me Dad had left.'

Pam looked worried. 'Shall I ask if she needs anything?'

'Such as what?'

'A cup of tea?'

Alone in the living room, I gazed at a photo of Mum and Dad on their wedding day. They both looked so young. This was pre-asymmetrical bob days, and Mum had long dark hair. In the picture, Dad appeared as thin as a rake, with a bum-fluff moustache and curly blonde hair. In his rented suit, he could have stepped out of Burtons's window.

Mum loved photos. Frames cluttered every surface. Spares ended up stored in albums, catalogued by date and lined up on dark-wooden bookcases. Yet, she disliked paintings or portraits. Mum's walls were covered with awards: Best Homemaker, Most Delicious Victoria Sponge, and Good Neighbour of the Year. And it didn't stop there; statuettes, plaques and silver salvos languished in a glass case.

How *could* she need anti-depressants? This was a woman who found silver linings in the darkest of clouds. If others argued the toss about glasses half full or half empty, she always saw a glass with room for more. Bad weather was an excuse to buy a new coat.

THE LIGHTS ARE ON

***

Pam popped her head back round the door.

'She'd like to talk to you. I'm making a pot of tea, but I need to nip next door. I've a box of fancies on their sell-by. Shame to waste them.'

I made my way up the stairs and stopped in front of the bedroom door. I wasn't sure whether to knock or walk right in. Luckily, she sensed my presence.

'Come in love,' she said.

They had propped mum up in bed, flour still in her hair, but otherwise less manic.

'I'm sorry about before,' she said. 'I gather I had one of my turns.'

'You were talking about Dad again.'

She rolled her eyes.

'You think I'd find someone more interesting when I'm away with the fairies.'

Despite everything, I laugh.

'You ought to get going,' she said as she swung her feet off the bed and into slippers. 'Won't your young man wonder where you've got to.'

'He's 56 Mum. *He* might be happy to hear you call him young. But he's not.'

She chuckled lightly and nodded agreement. 'I'm not sure what to say to you about all of that…'

***

She makes it sound like my coming out was recent. It's been thirty-two years. The clues had been there - my rejection of football and the way I posed Action Man dolls - engaged in boy-on-boy action, pubic hair drawn in black biro.

I chose Friday teatime for the big announcement, right after Mum came back from the chippie with a fish supper.

'I've got something to tell you,' I said and reached for a pickled onion. 'I'm gay.'

Dad said little, but Mum burst into tears.

'I'm to blame,' she said between sobs. 'I should have made you go to boy scouts more often.'

I didn't dare tell her that my first real sexual encounter was a curious fumble with on a scouting trip to Wales.

* * *

'Why don't you come back to mine,' I said. 'Mike is making pasta. He always does too much.'

She screwed up her nose. 'I've a slice of mushroom quiche in the fridge.'

'He'd love to see you.'

Mum looked less sure of herself. 'Did you tell him about today?'

'Of course not.'

She shrugged. 'I won't stop over this time, but dinner would be nice. The quiche will last until tomorrow.'

Pam opened the front door. 'It's only me' she trilled.

'Oh Jesus,' Mum sighed. 'Will she ever leave me in peace?'

'I think she's got out-of-date cake to force on you.'

Downstairs Pam had laid out shop-worn cake on a plate and set it on a tray. She was busy arranging a carnation into a tiny china vase. 'Nearly ready,' she smiled. 'Your mother loves flowers. Where does she keeps the doilies?'

'She's on her way down.'

'Is that wise?'

'I'm taking her back to mine for the night.'

Pam looked relieved. 'I hoped you might.'

* * *

Mike did his best not to sound narked when I called to say we were on our way. 'That'll be brilliant,' he said in a voice that suggested anything but.

'She's been talking about Dad again.'

'Oh,' he said simply. 'I'm sorry.'

Mum insisted on driving and that meant me spending much of the way there with my eyes tight closed. How she avoided a major pile up, I didn't know. She only ever looked left at junctions and traffic lights proved optional.

I poured myself a stiff drink as she toured the garden, dead-heading roses.

'Have you called her nurse?' Mike said.

'We spoke to the family doctor.'

'The Polish troll.'

'He gave her antidepressants.'

Mike shook his head. 'Didn't you say anything?'

'What was there to say? She gets like this because she killed her husband and I helped bury him in the back garden.'

Mum came in from the cold. 'One of you must have green fingers. My own back garden is a mess. I must get someone in to sort it out.'

'No,' I say perhaps too quickly. 'Remember the badgers.'

She looked annoyed. 'How come I'm the only one in the street they bother? I've been looking and I think they might have moved on.'

'The man from the council said it needs to be six years with no sign of settlement,' I say.

She tuts. 'What do they know?'

'Go wash your hands if you've been messing with roses,' I say. 'Dinner is nearly done.'

***

The evening when Mum killed Dad was one of the rare occasions when the whole family was getting on great. We'd all had a few glasses of wine. Mike was playing guitar and Mum sang along. Dad had been messing with the barbecue, poking at the coals, telling us it still wasn't hot enough for the steaks to go on.

She hit him with a champagne bottle. At first he turned cross-eyed and stumbled a little, so she hit him again. And then again and when he fell to the floor, one more time. That was when it shattered.

'He was sleeping with Pam,' she said. 'I caught them in bed together.'

Mike was the first to suggest an ambulance.

'I doubt they'll be of any use,' she said. 'I suppose I best start the steaks. The coals look hot enough.'

I wanted to call the police, but Mike stopped me. 'She's not well,' he said.

My hands were shaking, and I wanted to be sick.

'She killed my father.'

'Perhaps she had good reason.'

'Are you fucking mad?'

'No, but she might well be.'

He talked me into waiting to see what happened next.

'Look at her,' he said. 'She's carrying on like nothing happened.'

Mum had placed a tea towel over Dad's face, and she was busy grilling sirloins.

'We should wait until she's calmer.' Mike said. 'Right now she could be a danger to herself and to you.'

'But not to you,' I said a little bitterly.

That's when Pam rang the doorbell.

'Jesus Christ, no,' I said and ran to get it. It took forever to talk her out of coming in to *have a quick word*.

'I think she caught a glimpse of something that needs to be explained,' Pam said. 'It wasn't how it seemed.'

Somehow I picked at dinner. Mum made us sit at the table and she poured wine. When everything was done, she tidied things away. 'We must so something with your father,' she said as she poured a kettle of water on the barbecue. 'He can't stop there.'

*　*　**

The next day was when she started with the stories of him walking out. Pam came round while I was in the back garden with Mike, hiding the body in the shed.

'What are we doing?' I said.

'Protecting a loved one.'

I looked up and saw Mum with Pam; they were watching us.

'Oh shitting hell,' I said and ran to find out what they had seen.

'Pam understands,' Mum said. 'She'll keep quiet.'

She was having a *window of lucidity.* She's had a fair few over the years. Doctors have studied her, she's been written up in the Lancet. Not bad going for someone who committed cold-blooded murder and somehow convinced a jury she was insane.

Mike helped me then, but with each burst of energy, our bond weakened. I sensed him move away.

'I might spend a few days with my folks,' he said as we watched TV together.

'You should,' Mum said. 'They must miss seeing you. I'm always glad to spend time with my lad.'

And so he drove away the next morning. Leaving me with her.

'I'll call when I get there,' he said.

We didn't kiss.

* * *

And so we rubbed along for days that turned into weeks and soon enough months. Now and then, I collected her clothes and opened our front door to papers, letters, bills and often cards from estate agents who swore they had ready buyers desperate to move into the area.

I called Mike.

'Are we done?' I said.

He left enough space between question and answer to tell me all I needed.

'What she did… what happened. I'm not sure we can ever…'

So I phoned someone. A nice enough man in a shiny suit came by and told me what a lovely home she had. I talked Mum into signing papers and he took care of viewings.

* * *

Mum played the piano. She'd sit in the back room and pick out notes. It could sound beautiful, it could sound like the most regret-soaked thing ever.

She never asked where Mike went and slowly stopped talking about Dad. My life changed too. I got used to her being there and learned to love the togetherness.

One night she told me she'd taken the bus across town. I'd been out buying food - a special dinner to mark her birthday.

'I ran into Pam,' she said.

A familiar headache took hold. 'What did you talk about?'

'She didn't actually see me. I hid. That time is over now.' Mum reached out for me and I held her hand. 'We'll be OK, won't we? Nobody is coming now?'

* * *

We never spoke again. I found her peaceful in her bed, eyes closed, a smile played across her lips. So much light still within. Nobody home.

Home again

There isn't a day goes by she doesn't nip over on some pretence or other. Yesterday it was to ask if I'd any dark palm sugar. The day before to ask if I'd hung onto last week's *Radio Times*. As if I'm the sort of person who hoards periodicals.

She imagines I came down in the last shower. I presume all she wants is to find out what went on. Perhaps I should put a notice in the Gazette.

"My son hung himself because he was ashamed of what you all thought he'd done. My son hung himself because he didn't want his mother to put up with doing time too. My son hung himself because of people like you."

Happy now?

I can't condemn her. I'd be the same.

Chrissie said, 'Mum, it's like you're a local celebrity.'

Fame costs, but no mother should pay this price.

Right after they brought your things round, it started. The prison governor came along personally. She looked better turned out than that night they called me in. I meant to ask where she got the coat. We're about the same size and build, and I'll need something black.

I've never bought a single item of dark clothing in my life. I've always avoided it. My mother used to haunt the shadows of her miserable terraced house dressed in black, and I swore to never be like that. Everyone tells me she used to be full of the joys of spring until our John died. I survived and was born. She had this way of making me believe it was my fault.

'We'll need you to sign this release form,' the governor said and watched while a chubby girl rummaged in a briefcase. She was all in black too. Big clumpy shoes, men's trousers, short dark hair, not a scrap of makeup. Seemed to have something against smiling.

It must be what they teach them.

When dealing with the relatives of the recently deceased, whatever you do, don't smile.

They gave me your stuff. Someone washed your clothes and ironed them and put everything in a carrier bag. They could have belonged to anybody. I'd never seen you in them.

The rest of your stuff was in a sealed envelope. I waited till they left before opening it.

I was careful and slid my nail under the flap and moved it from side to side. I didn't want to tear the paper.

The watch was the one we got for your sixteenth birthday. You'd been dropping hints for weeks. Your father said it was too much to pay, but I'd put money aside and told him there was a sale on in town. The woman in the shop was a snooty piece. She took one look at me and said something about how they didn't give change for the bus. When I handed over the money, she didn't want to touch it, and I bet she slipped through the back to wash her hands afterwards.

I walked past the shop the other day and she's still there. Same sour old face.

Your ring. Silver. Tarnished. Like the coins you used to keep in that old tin box. One afternoon I came home and found you'd covered them in tomato sauce. Something you'd seen on Blue Peter. It brought them up lovely, but your father hit the roof.

He had to have his chips with brown sauce.

I didn't dare look in your wallet yet.

* * *

The vicar came round straight after the governor left, and I told him about the form. He said something about the Lord being there for me and offered to pray for us.

I said that was kind and made a cup of tea.

Why is it that everybody says they know how you feel?

If I had a pound for everyone who'd dispensed their words of wisdom by telling me they appreciated what I must go through, I wouldn't need to buy another scratch card.

The thing is, they *don't* know how I feel.

They don't.

Then came the social worker.

Skinny little bloke, thick-rimmed glasses, greasy hair. Wouldn't take his coat off.

I made him tea as well and let him babble on.

He finished half a pack of digestives. I've no idea where he put it all. He was as thin as a rake.

At first I thought we'd get through it together. Keith did everything to make sure I didn't have to deal with the paperwork and stuff. He helped me plan the funeral and the wake.

That went off well.

Most of his so-called friends and family only came to gawp, but I made sure the drink flowed, and someone took to the piano to play *"Danny Boy"*. All things considered, it was a good day. I found myself daring to smile.

And then *she* phoned and asked to come round.

Keith said to tell her to sling her hook.

I should have done.

She wasn't at all like I'd expected. I'd go so far as to say she was a pleasant little thing, with short blondish hair, although there was barely a picking of meat on her bones. That's the thing with young people these days. They see it all on YouTube and they want to be the same. They starve themselves and chuck up food in toilets. It's immoral when you consider the kiddies in Africa.

I had to keep asking her to speak up, and half hoped she'd come to tell me she was carrying your child. Just like in the soaps. It's funny how you can have these big blousy confident women who go through their lives sleeping with every chap that comes their way and the second anything bad happens, they end up pregnant.

That wasn't why she came.

Part of me wanted her to say how you'd been seeing each other for a while and that this had all been a mistake. That it was only because her Mam found out that there'd been all this trouble.

That wasn't why she came.

She spoke in a flat voice, like someone who'd forgotten how to smile. I'm ashamed to say, but I tuned her out. I found myself running through my shopping list and trying to remember if this was the week to put out the green bin.

What ever did you see in her?

It crossed my mind to ask what she was doing down the park on her own. At that time of night. Asking for trouble.

I didn't.

When she left, she said she'd like to come round again. Her eyes stared into mine and her lips tried to smile. She held my hands as if we were important to each other.

'We can talk more,' she said. 'I'd like that.'

I told her I'd rather she stayed away, and she looked upset.

It must not have come out right.

I planned on telling her I hadn't meant it to sound cruel, but decided to just let her go.

So now I'm busy grappling with *'neighbourhood witch'* as Keith calls them. Curtain twitchers who pop in twice a day to make sure I'm coping. They offer to do my shopping or run a duster up the bannisters.

They treat me like an invalid.

The thing is, I can't bring myself to face the world yet.

If I stay right here and do nothing, I might wake up and find it was all a dream. And that would be lovely. To find out, I mean, not the dream. It wouldn't be lovely at all. More like a nightmare.

I was listening to Radio 4 the other afternoon. One of those plays they put on to pass the day. I must have fallen asleep, because next thing, it had finished and instead I heard the end of a phone-in. They were talking about you. One woman said she blamed the parents.

'They're the ones who ought to go to jail,' she said. 'They're the ones to punish.'

I used to think, how can you kill someone with kindness?

That isn't possible, surely.

Now I'm not so sure.

* * *

The doctor came by yesterday. At least that's who she said she was. I've never seen her before. She could have been anyone.

I miss Doctor Hill.

This new woman kept looking at her watch and telling me how busy she was. She wrote out a prescription for tablets.

I said I'd get someone to fetch them.

It's still behind the clock. With your wallet.

* * *

Here she comes again. She said she'd call in after tea to make sure I was OK. That's why I've turned off the lights. Maybe she'll think I've had an early night Any second now she'll knock on the door and call through the letterbox.

I'll pretend I fell asleep and say it's a good job she came round. We'll end up watching Coronation Street together.

Tomorrow will be different. I'm taking you out for the day. We'll do the things we used to do, the things we should have done more often.

I can't honestly make up for turning a blind eye to what was going on back then, but you have to see how it was for me.

He was my husband. I took certain vows.

You kids don't bother with that sort of thing, but we did.

I suppose I better put something on for tea.

I like it in the dark, on my own.

When there's nobody around, when there's nobody to chat to, nothing to

see, I can still tell myself it never happened.
　The phone rings, and someone knocks on the door.
　Nobody can say I'm lonely.
　I've you to thank for that.

3AM

The damp patch in the room's corner has got bigger. It's obvious even in the half light. Now it looks like Africa, or am I thinking of South America? The pointy one anyway. Or are they both pointy?

Definitely not Australia. That's more oval. And Lucy lives right near the bottom on the right.

In Melbourne.

It'll be the middle of the afternoon there and I suppose she'll be at work. I ought to email. Something casual. A 'how are you doing?' mail.

3AM exists for a reason. It's when I do my best worrying.

There's a lump on my leg and I don't know how it came about. It's been there a week now and ought to go down. There's no bruising, just this soggy lumpy bit of me attached to my leg. I looked online, and it turns out it's either an infection, rheumatoid arthritis or terminal cancer.

Not that cancers run in our family. Terminal or otherwise. Strokes tend to see us off.

And heart attacks.

Except for my uncle Reggie. He got hit by a car. It was his own fault. The stubborn sod was 90 and refused to use the footpath. Used to say he was here before the cars. The kid driving was only 17. His family sent flowers.

I looked in the mirror this morning. Really looked. Not a quick check for nose hair look. A proper examination. With the lights on.

God, I'm looking old.

And I'm losing my hair. I've always had a big forehead, they used to call me Slaphead at school. But I'm sure it's receding. I hope I'm not losing it on top too. I've no idea what's going on there. When I have my hair cut, I always laugh when the barber picks up a mirror and offers to show me the back.

'It's OK,' I say. 'I trust you.'

I'm already going grey. Louise at work reckons it's sexy.

'You're looking distinguished, Simon,' she said the other day. 'Look at Philip Schofield.'

Distinguished is another word for old.

It's OK if you spend your mornings laughing at strange-shaped vegetables on a sofa. You can have your hair whatever colour you like. When you work in a bank, stick with the hand you're dealt.

Flash Dan from IT support uses Grecian 2000. You can tell. It looks like he combed boot polish through his hair.

And he drives a Porsche.

Tosser.

'Why would anyone fancy Dan?' I once asked his colleague, Lucy.

'I suppose it's his personality,' she managed eventually.

'Nothing to do with the Porsche?'

'That's just something men *think* makes them look good. Women find it funny.'

It didn't stop her from letting him snog her at the Christmas party. She thought I didn't see, but I did. They both pretended to be drunk, but I'd heard tell Tom he was on antibiotics so he couldn't drink.

I could get up and go to the gym. It's open 24 hours a day and you only need to put your pin code in. I've always wondered what sort of people go in the middle of the night.

Sad bastards with no life.

So what does that make me?

They've had this extra room built with machines that do your whole workout in half an hour or something. I must see what it's all about. Tom reckons it's brilliant.

Christ! Tom.

I really ought to ring him back.

He keeps leaving messages.

He sounded pissed off in the last one.

'Call me back if you remember my number.'

The thing is, he's not to know why I've been avoiding him. One erotic dream about your best mate doesn't make you gay. Even if *he* is.

But three? That's got to mean something.

And *I'm* not.

Gay, that is.

I've been engaged twice, booked a church once, even got as far as agreeing the order of service before she decided marriage was 'this enormous step, right? What if we're not ready? What if we're not those people? What if somewhere out there, there's someone else we're both meant to be with and we have kids and end up messing with their heads?'

Close escape, that one.

Last time I heard anything of Lucy, she was being evicted from Dale Farm. Tom reckoned he saw her on the news throwing half a house brick at a police car.

I ought to ring him back. I will do.

Tomorrow.

Or Saturday maybe.

And suggest we meet up. For drinks. Perhaps a game of pool. Dinner. Whatever.

3AM is the perfect time to worry about cancer.

My current favourite obsessions are prostrate and testicular.

It bothers me I might not be doing the examination right.

I downloaded an episode of *This Morning* where they had a doctor showing men how to examine their balls and I'm sure there was some kind of a lump the first time, but then try as I might I couldn't track it down again.

I ought to go to the doctor, but it's murder getting an appointment unless your head's hanging off. And that bitch on reception wants to know everything before she'll agree to let you sit on one of the chairs in reception.

I ought to go private, but it goes against everything I believe in politically. I took it out of Tom when he told me he'd signed up for BUPA. I can hardly back down now.

Not to mention how much it costs.

I had to cancel my AA cover last month.

It can only be days before the car breaks down.

And nobody wants to tell you how to examine yourself for prostrate cancer. I've tried the Internet, but it all seems graphic and hideous. Not that I've got any problems with sticking a finger up my bum. Like I say, I'm perfectly comfortable with my sexuality.

On the whole.

Apart from that dream.

Though thinking about it, I had a bag of cheesy Wotsits before bed last night and they never really agree with me.

So here I am, going bald, possibly riddled with hidden cancers and single. Having homo-erotic dreams and worrying about money. Is it any wonder my hair is falling out and I look so old?

Maddy turns over, her eyes wide open to transmit anger.

'Are you ever going to stop typing?' she says and swipes at the lamp on our bedside table. 'What are you working on now?'

'A piece about getting old?' I say. 'I'm not sure how to end it.'

'Can you have someone die?'

'Done it too much.'

'Wake up and find it was all a dream.'

'I might just have them roll over and have sex,' I say hopefully. She gives me a look that suggests it's not my lucky night.

'Make yourself a milky drink and turn that bloody iPad off.'

I nod and do as she says, only to watch the numbers change on my clock.

At 4am, I'm downstairs and waiting for the kettle to boil. Not that I fancy tea, but what else is there? I can hardly open a bottle of wine at this time of night. Or rather, early morning. I'd be pissed by breakfast. And that's a slippery slope.

Maddy gets up and flushes the toilet. Like she always does at 4.15. She doesn't come down to see if I'm OK.

I suppose we *do* still love each other. She infuriates me just as much as I drive her insane. That we still feel something must count. Pale indifference would be tragic.

The first birds sing and I prop open the back door, enjoying the cool air of dawn. Soon the chorus grows optimistic and full. I rinse my cup, lock the back door, and climb the stairs.

Maddy hardly stirs as I slide back into bed. I kiss her shoulder and she brushes me away.

Daylight seeps around the curtains and each dark worry, fear and doubt loses power. For now. Until it's 3AM tomorrow, when I'll dig again until answers come.

December

Outside it's snowing, and it hasn't had the usual effect. Normally, I'd be decking the halls with boughs of holly but this year, my primary worry is slipping over on ice and doing myself an injury.

I'm either getting old or it's the after-effects of one of the most spectacular runs of bad luck going.

I'm fairly used to the odd mishap now and then. It wouldn't be real life if everything ran smoothly.

I *expect* to lose umbrellas, scuff favourite shoes and spill cups of tea over white sofas (Top Tip alert, - Don't bother with stain removers; if it's white and stained use Mr Muscle oven cleaner - works a treat). But the last six weeks have been exceptional even by my standards.

It all started when the cold weather set in at the start of November. Mr Fanning cranked up the heating. But nothing happened. Our boiler had lost the will.

Repair man after repairman did sharp intakes of breath and offered to take money to '*do what they could.*' Each issued dire warnings that any repair would be temporary.

I took temporary to mean it would last through the winter. They didn't.

What they meant was that by the time they were tucked up in some gezellig Dutch café, the Fanning household would shiver once more in sub-Arctic conditions.

After a week of trading insults around a one-bar electric fire and washing with a bucket of lukewarm water, we gave in and shelled out for a replacement.

Then the fridge went wild and decided that keeping things cold wasn't nearly enough. *All* food should be frozen *at all times*.

Lettuce, milk, it didn't discriminate.

Cue another patronising Mr Fixit (*"oh dear, it's two seconds out of guarantee"*) and another bill.

Things go in threes; so when Mr Fanning called to say the computer had exploded in a post-Guy Fawkes cloud of sparks, my response was muted acceptance.

Of course it had.

I arrived home to the set of a late 70s horror film. Lights flickered and shorted. Toasters, kettles and popcorn makers (I was stoned, the salesman was cute) randomly emitted pops and small clouds of white smoke.

By the time everything was switched off, we were down one washing machine (expensive), one satellite box (outrageously expensive), one iMac (prohibitive), not to mention a kettle and some contraption that controlled the garage door.

Cue more repairs and, to sweeten the pot, Dutch insurance forms.

* * *

Mr Fanning developed a series of colds and throat infections. He never said so much, but I knew he wanted it to be swine flu. Just so he could tell everyone he'd had it.

Like all buffoons, I consulted the Internet.

He had the cough, the sore throat, the runny nose and aching joints. But what of his temperature? It had to be above 38 degrees to qualify.

I rushed to our local chemist–one of the most miserable places on God's earth (which is a shame, since I've always quite liked chemists, but our local is staffed by humourless ghouls).

Mr Fanning took the thermometer.

He sat and waited the requisite two minutes.

Together, we peered at the result. 37.4.

Officially, nothing more than an awful cold.

I could tell he was disappointed by the way he kept checking every hour to see if things had changed.

The next day, satisfied he wouldn't die if left alone, I set out for the office. Hours later, my mobile rang. It was Mr Fanning, beside himself with excitement.

'I've done it, I'm 38.2,' he bragged.

I was so proud.

Then I caught it and my competitive streak took over. I only ever managed 37.6–which, although I felt ghastly, is apparently normal.

I did however trump Mr F by putting my back out not once, but twice, necessitating the sort of painkillers that could fell a grizzly bear - and several days off work watching daytime TV (and slowly losing the will to live).

Who has that much crap in their attic, and why can't the owners of said crap blow their profits on a decent night at the pub?

Why does there always have to be a dying relative, or a disabled child with their heart set on an exchange visit to Lourdes?

The long and short of all this is that I'm feeling old. Maybe I've finally reached the age where I'll always have something wrong. When people stop me in the street and ask how I'm keeping, I'll be able to regale them with tales of my latest ailment. Part of me likes this.

Reunion - A Christmas Story

You'd be late for your own funeral. That's what Emily's mother used to say. Years of burned dinners, missed appointments and parking tickets end here. This Christmas.

She's made a list. She's checked it twice.

Everything is ready for the best family Christmas ever. It's taken three shopping trips to get everything.

They'll arrive at seven. Or so they said. That's more than enough time to get the house looking ship-shape. This year, she won't scrabble in the loft for a tired tinsel tree while the turkey thaws in the bath. She got the tree down yesterday and stuck it together with plumbing tape. There's enough ribbons and baubles to hide running repairs.

'Everyone's dressing their trees in white,' Sophie told her last year. 'You really ought to consider a real tree next time.'

'They make too much mess,' Emily said. 'And this one has been in the family since you were born.'

Her daughter exchanged looks with her husband. Chinless James. The bored bank manager who sleeps with his secretary.

'I think it's lovely,' he said, and that's when Emily decided this year *would* be different.

The presents are wrapped in silver and gold.

Sophie and James promised to call on their way to the airport. Two weeks in the sun. Away from the cold, the slush and the rain and wind that whistles around loose-fitting panes in kitchen windows.

'I don't know if I could enjoy a turkey dinner when it's hot outside,' Emily said when Sophie announced the plans.

'We'll probably have sushi by the pool.'

'Sushi for Christmas dinner? What about the kids? Won't they miss Santa?'

'Lauren and Harry are staying with Barbara.'

Emily forced a smile to stay put. 'That'll be nice for them. They *ought* to spend more time with their other grandma.'

'We've had to promise to bring back a crate of local wine.'

'You can get me some too,' Emily said and laughed, but Sophie didn't answer.

The Stourbridge crystal looks lovely. Today feels like a day for the best glasses. And champagne. The good stuff she keeps hidden behind John's lawnmower in the garage. It's been waiting for an occasion. The plastic centrepiece summons thoughts of a wintry afternoon back when Sophie and Ben were six. They'd taken the dogs for a walk. It was freezing cold. Ben chucked sticks and Holly helped gather mistletoe.

Back home, the kids ran to find John.

'Look what we found, Dad,' Sophie said. 'Kiss me now.'

John put down his newspaper and laughed. How she missed that. How she missed him, but there's no time to think of that now. It's time to get changed. The white dress has hung on the back of the door since Tuesday. It still fits after all these years.

Emily's made a list. Now she's checking it twice.

She won't need shoes. Or lipstick. Or the wig. She recalls how John would fasten her necklace and let his lips linger. How he'd whisper something filthy and suggest they stay home.

'Let's make an excuse.'

'I promised Sophie.'

'She'll be busy with her fancy friends. I can't face a room of bank managers.'

'They've gone to a lot of trouble.'

'It'll be things on sticks and you know that won't fill me up. We'll stop for chips on the way home.'

Emily laughed and turned her head to taste his mouth. Stale wine, edged with brandy. And cigarettes.

'Have you been smoking?'

'I only had one.'
'You promised.'
John pulled away. 'I only had one.'

* * *

The phone rings. She lets the machine pick up. It's Sophie. As expected, with this year's excuse. 'Mum are you there? Pick up.'

A short pause, then the line goes dead. That's a turn up for the book. She's coming after all. It makes things so much better. Reunions can be tricky when half the people don't show. In a few short hours, the doorbell will sing *"White Christmas"*. The man in the pound shop laughed when she bought it.

'That'll drive you mad by Boxing Day,' he said.

She didn't tell him she was halfway there already.

The cork leaves the bottle with a satisfying pop. John taught her how to open champagne. Turn the bottle not the cork. She last drank champagne on the day they said she was in remission. They'd taken away the lump and expected her to be happy. It didn't seem to matter that they'd taken away her hair and her smile.

'To the future,' John said. And if she'd had any idea how short that future would be, she'd have drunk it slowly.

* * *

When the car left the road, time grew sticky. Lights drifted past the windows. Ben cried out and John's hand found hers as his face fell apart. Ben was next. He lay there, out of reach on the back seat. Sobbing, then wheezing.

Then nothing.

* * *

Emily opens the kitchen drawer and pulls out three silver-wrapped boxes. One for Sophie. One for Ben and one for John. It's time. One by one.

Each white tablet washed away with fine champagne.

Sophie and James will be on their way by now. The phone rings again. Surely not. She wished she'd got one of those machines that showed the number. Her outgoing message plays and then Sophie speaks. 'We wanted to see you before we went,' she says. 'But it's been on the radio, the M25 is rammed and if we leave it any later, we could miss our flight and then you'd be stuck with us for Christmas.'

Emily smiles first at John, then at Ben. Some things never change. Some things you can count on.

It won't be long now.

A last-minute gift

The tree is up, the cupboards groan with food, but Josie can't bring herself to feel it. The thought of Christmas fills her with dread.

Everybody at work was full of cheer. And she joined in, wearing last year's reindeer jumper and helping with the bake sale. It's three weeks to the day she took her best friend for his last walk. Tomorrow will be the first Christmas Day in sixteen years without Bertie.

She's downloaded *A Wonderful Life*. It will make her cry, but Josie hopes it might kick-start the Christmas thing. She'll watch it with the lights off and a box of supermarket mince pies.

If she keeps the room dark, Bertie is still here. In the basket she's not yet moved from in front of the fire, filling the room with his malted milk sleep smells.

The weather has been typically Christmas. Rainy and dull, but as this short afternoon wore on, the sun broke through grey clouds and bathed the garden in a beautiful light. Josie glanced at Bertie's lead, still hanging on the back of the door. Around about now, she'd rattle her keys, and he'd leap from his basket to dance a jig at her feet.

She missed the walks. Almost as much as she missed Bertie. Even though Josie lived alone and didn't mix with the people from work, she had dog walking friends. They'll have noticed her absence. Did they guess that Bertie had gone?

Why shouldn't she go out?

***

Josie heads through the woods and smiles as she pictures Bertie snuffling his way along the path. She nods hello to Schnauzer Elaine and Labrador Bill. She can't bring herself to stop and chat, because they'll want to know about Bertie.

Up ahead, someone sits on a bench. No dog at their side. As she gets closer, she realises that it's Poodle Pete.

'Hello lovely lady,' he says, and shuffles over for Josie to sit.

Any minute Stinker will come rushing through the bushes, *haa-haa-*ing his way through long grass, chasing a squirrel. She's not sure she can cope with pretending there's nothing wrong.

'Are you all sorted for Christmas Day?' she says and he nods.

'My Maureen has bankrupted us, and for what? It's only a big dinner.'

They sit in silence for a while, and when there's no sign of Stinker, she's forced to ask.

'Are you alone?'

He nods and Josie's heart bursts. How could two of the loveliest boys ever leave this world at the same time?

'I'm sorry,' she says, and overwhelmed by sadness gets to her feet. 'I best head home, it'll be dark soon.'

'Three girls and a boy,' Pete says. 'I don't suppose you fancy seeing them?'

* * *

Stinker is the most attentive father. He fusses around Labrador Molly like he knows she's unsure where the four little hungry balls of fluff came from.

'They're beautiful,' Josie says.

'That little white one,' Pete says. 'I bet he reminds you of someone.'

He does, and Josie has been doing her best not to say anything. She's only got the one picture of Bertie as a pup. He grew up so fast after he left the dog's home.

'We can't keep them,' Pete says. 'So I suppose come the new year, it's adoption time.'

All at once, Josie knows she's feeling Christmas. She looks around Pete's front room, taking in the tree, the twinkling lights, the crackling logs on the open fire. The smell of something lovely wafting from the kitchen.

'I could take him,' she says, and then quickly adds. 'That's if you don't mind.'

* * *

Josie sips her sherry in the flickering light of the television screen. She smiles over at Bertie's empty basket. In six short weeks, it will belong to someone new.

'You don't mind, lad?' she says.

And somewhere, far away she hears him barking.

Or maybe it was the wind.

She can't be sure.

'Merry Christmas, old boy.'

The beating of a thousand wings

It's a sound I've heard before. The beating of a thousand wings.

Aged six, I held Dad's hand and watched the swallows swoop. When I asked where they were going, he said France and it sounded so far away. His watery eyes peer into the January sky.

'That's France,' I say.

I know he wants to tell me that France is too far away to see from up here, and that I'm such a stupid kid. If only I'd paid attention at school, I might have a proper job. But they took away his voice along with the first of the cancer.

I wrapped the blanket round his shoulders, and his face brushed against my hand.

'Maybe that's where they'll find you,' I said, and I'm sure he nodded.

Gulls peck at dirty ground; their cries remind me of weeks in Devon. The four of us in the car. My sister on alert, determined to be first to spot the sea.

Days on the beach, evenings in the caravan.

Her voice in the night as she begged you to stop. Again and again.

'It's why I brought you here, Dad.'

You already know how to release the brake, and I suppose you'll do it when you've made your peace with whatever God you pray to these days.

'Goodbye.'

A voice on the car radio warns of storms and high winds.

The beating of a thousand wings

It's a sound I've heard before.

This is not America

Rose cringed when Betty spoke. She tried her level best not to, but sweet Jesus, life with her was tough.

'We're from Daytona,' she said. 'You heard of it?'

The guy shook his head. Every guy did. Didn't matter none because Betty made it her business to fill that knowledge gap.

'It's the lawnmower capital of America,' she said proudly. This was where she almost always paused and waited for a reaction. It never came.

'We've got a museum and everything.'

This used to be Betty's line, but Rose stole it. She delivered it with a sarcastic inflection so folk understood she wasn't bragging.

'Right,' said the guy who only stopped out of politeness. He probably saw two aging broads lost in the center of Paris.

'You a Brit?' Rose said.

'Well, yes.'

Betty took back over. 'I love your country. I adore everything about it. It's so… historic.'

She pronounced the 'h'. Rose believed this to be wrong.

Betty had her arm through his. She led him away to a bench under a tree. The poor guy. He probably had places to be.

'I never dreamed that one day I'd get to enjoy the Mona Lisa in person,' she was saying.

'The French call her La Gioconda.'

'Really? Hey Rose. Did you hear? That broad in the picture, her real name ain't Lisa.'

'It may have been,' their new friend blurted. 'I'm only telling you what the French call her. Nobody knows her actual name.'

'Ah crap,' Betty laughed. 'I thought you might tell me a secret.'

Rose noticed how she placed her hand onto his arm. Surely not. They'd had enough of trouble.

'What was your name again?' Betty said.

'Christopher.'

'What a noble name. I guess you must get asked this all the time. Are you related to the Queen of England?'

'Oh, goodness no.'

'Hey. You never know. You might be. You look royal, you got regal eyes. Rose come see this guy's eyes. Do they remind you of someone?'

Rose played along. She peered into his face and offered a sympathetic smile. 'Forgive my friend. We slept little last night. Jet lag.'

'It's fine,' he said.

'He looks like Prince Charles,' Betty insisted.

Rose looked again. 'Yeah, I see it now.'

Christopher stared past them and whistled and waved. A guy with floppy dark hair glanced around.

'That's my friend Jonathan,' he said. 'We're traveling together.'

Betty leaned in to whisper. 'You guys together?'

'Yes, like I said, we're traveling through Europe.'

'No.' She shook her head. 'I mean *together*.'

In case there was any doubt, she managed the most theatrical of winks.

'Goodness me no,' he said and jumped up to shake his friend's hand. 'Johnny boy. This charming lady thinks we're a pair of fruits.'

Betty roared with laughter and Rose felt mortified.

'Ooh ducky,' the new guy affected a fey voice. 'Never turn your back on me then.'

Christopher didn't laugh.

'Why don't we all go for tea?'

'Tea?' said Betty. 'How wonderfully British.'

Jonathan shook his head. 'It's five o'clock. Tea at this hour would be vulgar.

This is *l'heure d'apéritif.*'

'Don't let us keep you,' Rose said and Betty looked furious.

'You should join us,' said Christopher.

Betty didn't need asking twice. She led the way, and it was only when they reached a bar that Rose pulled her to one side.

'We *can't* do this,' she said. 'What if we get caught?'

'This is not America,' Betty laughed. 'All bets are off.'

* * *

Christopher ordered cocktails. Champagne with some strawberry thing in it. Rose's head swam. She should have eaten.

'To new friends,' Betty proposed a toast. 'And fresh memories.'

Jonathan whispered something in her ear. Sensing danger Rose suggested they retire to the restrooms.

'What did he whisper?' she asked as Betty washed her hands.

'He wants me to go to his room.'

'You can't.'

'Why ever not? A handsome man takes pleasure in my company. Who am I to deny him?'

'And what about me?'

'You are welcome to Christopher.'

'He's a gentleman.'

'Yeah, that's what I surmised. Bad luck.'

'We should move on.'

Betty looked up from the sink. Her eyes grew cold.

'We can't get far without money.'

Back at the table, Jonathan had ordered cognac.

'Taste this,' he said when the women sat. 'It's over a hundred years old.'

This time it was Christopher who excused himself.

'Out of my depth,' he said. 'Keep my seat warm.'

Nobody but Rose noticed when Betty spiked Jonathan's drink.

Whatever she used soon took effect and Betty suggested a walk by the Seine.

Jonathan's eyes looked bloodshot and his speech became slurred. Christopher laughed.

'Not quite the hardcore drinker you claim to be, eh?'

'You should accompany him home,' said Rose.

Betty cut in.

'You two enjoy your drink. I got this. He'll get into a taxi.'

Rose nodded. What other choice was there?

'We'll order black coffee,' said Christopher when they were alone. 'Sort out our heads.'

The hours ambled. Rose tuned out conversation and nodded and smile at appropriate points. Her only concern was Betty. She knew what she could do. The last time was the last time, she'd said. Now less than 24 hours later, here they were again.

'I need air,' she said eventually. 'Would you mind if I took five minutes?'

'Of course,' said Christopher. 'I'll be waiting.'

Around the corner, out of sight, she called Betty's phone. There was no answer, just voice mail.

'Come back,' she said. 'We need to leave Paris.'

When she stepped inside, her heart tumbled.

The waiter was at their table. He looked around and called for help.

Christopher's eyes were closed and his head tipped to one side, his tongue hung out.

'Madame,' the waiter cried when he spotted her. 'Your friend is sick.'

Blue lights flashed, the ambulance arrived. And then the police. They asked questions about how she met Christopher. And then wanted to ask about her friend. Where was this woman she called Rose?

'Your passport is a forgery,' said the weedy gendarme.

Betty nodded. 'Rose stole mine.'

'There's no record of either of you at the hotel you told me about.'

He shrugged. The most Gallic of gestures.

* * *

This is *l'heure d'apéritif.*

'Don't let us keep you,' Rose said and Betty looked furious.

'You should join us,' said Christopher.

Betty didn't need asking twice. She led the way, and it was only when they reached a bar that Rose pulled her to one side.

'We *can't* do this,' she said. 'What if we get caught?'

'This is not America,' Betty laughed. 'All bets are off.'

* * *

Christopher ordered cocktails. Champagne with some strawberry thing in it. Rose's head swam. She should have eaten.

'To new friends,' Betty proposed a toast. 'And fresh memories.'

Jonathan whispered something in her ear. Sensing danger Rose suggested they retire to the restrooms.

'What did he whisper?' she asked as Betty washed her hands.

'He wants me to go to his room.'

'You can't.'

'Why ever not? A handsome man takes pleasure in my company. Who am I to deny him?'

'And what about me?'

'You are welcome to Christopher.'

'He's a gentleman.'

'Yeah, that's what I surmised. Bad luck.'

'We should move on.'

Betty looked up from the sink. Her eyes grew cold.

'We can't get far without money.'

Back at the table, Jonathan had ordered cognac.

'Taste this,' he said when the women sat. 'It's over a hundred years old.'

This time it was Christopher who excused himself.

'Out of my depth,' he said. 'Keep my seat warm.'

Nobody but Rose noticed when Betty spiked Jonathan's drink.

Whatever she used soon took effect and Betty suggested a walk by the Seine.

Jonathan's eyes looked bloodshot and his speech became slurred. Christopher laughed.

'Not quite the hardcore drinker you claim to be, eh?'

'You should accompany him home,' said Rose.

Betty cut in.

'You two enjoy your drink. I got this. He'll get into a taxi.'

Rose nodded. What other choice was there?

'We'll order black coffee,' said Christopher when they were alone. 'Sort out our heads.'

The hours ambled. Rose tuned out conversation and nodded and smile at appropriate points. Her only concern was Betty. She knew what she could do. The last time was the last time, she'd said. Now less than 24 hours later, here they were again.

'I need air,' she said eventually. 'Would you mind if I took five minutes?'

'Of course,' said Christopher. 'I'll be waiting.'

Around the corner, out of sight, she called Betty's phone. There was no answer, just voice mail.

'Come back,' she said. 'We need to leave Paris.'

When she stepped inside, her heart tumbled.

The waiter was at their table. He looked around and called for help.

Christopher's eyes were closed and his head tipped to one side, his tongue hung out.

'Madame,' the waiter cried when he spotted her. 'Your friend is sick.'

Blue lights flashed, the ambulance arrived. And then the police. They asked questions about how she met Christopher. And then wanted to ask about her friend. Where was this woman she called Rose?

'Your passport is a forgery,' said the weedy gendarme.

Betty nodded. 'Rose stole mine.'

'There's no record of either of you at the hotel you told me about.'

He shrugged. The most Gallic of gestures.

***

Two days later the first body turned up. Along with Rose's passport. No matter how much she pleaded with them, they ignored her words.

'There must be records. CCTV. At the airport?'

'We have already checked.'

'And you saw us?'

'The system failed to record either of your arrivals.'

'We flew in on Saturday.'

'You're not on the airline manifest.'

'I used a fake passport. We both did.'

'It isn't looking good madam.'

***

They called her *The Angel of Death*. A girl, barely out of her teens came to visit, she wanted to tell Rose's story.

'I'm not the guilty one,' she said. The same line she'd repeated for four long years.

'I've spoken with Betty,' she said when the guards left them alone.

Rose raised her head. 'So she's still alive?'

'She wants you to forgive her.'

Rose laughed. 'I spent my last years in a French prison accused of two murders I didn't commit.'

'And three you did.'

She looked swiftly away. 'So you have been in touch with her?'

'She has a new life now. A fresh identity. She struck a deal for information.'

'She told them about the things that happened in Daytona?'

'Rose blamed someone else. You're not involved.'

Betty thought for a moment. The only person who came out of this looking good was the evil witch who caused the hurt. It was Rose who told her to go home that day and when Betty found Ronald in bed with Diane, something took over. Diane's sister was collateral damage. Unfortunate, given the situation, what choice did she have?

'My husband,' she said, and the girl shook her head.

'I already know what happened.'

'Don't shoot the messenger,' Betty said. 'That's what they say, isn't it?'

'I guess.'

'That's exactly who I should have aimed the gun at. She knew for so long. She let it grow. She let them carry on hurting me. She only told me when she realized it would hurt. I don't get why.'

The girl reached into her pocket and produced a photo. It was Rose. She'd had work done. She looked dignified but different. And the building in the background was familiar.

'That was my house,' Betty said. 'I don't understand.'

'You need to see this.'

The newspaper cutting told of how a woman uncovered the truth. Of how her friend killed three people in a fit of temper and then forced her to fly to Europe. Where she killed again. Twice.

'How did she get my house?'

'Don't you get it?' The girl said with a sigh. 'Rose killed no one. Betty did it all.'

Lucky Day

Barney Davis saluted single magpies, stroked black cats and rarely trod on sidewalk cracks. Yet his wife walked out when the bank took back the house. Two weeks after his supervisor told him ever-so-nicely that he was out of a job.

On the day he discovered the cash, every instinct said to hand it in. It waited in bushes near the park gates. Not especially well-concealed. He carried the sack to his truck and sat there, until common sense won over, and he hid it in the trunk.

Barney went back into the park to see if someone came searching for the cash. Nobody did. Maybe his find was drugs money.

In his head he took it to the cops, and someone leaked his story to the newspapers. They sent a guy round to take photos and all his neighbors Tweeted about him being a modern-day hero.

And that is what he should have done. But who would miss a few bucks? He needed a haircut.

The guy at the barbershop didn't blink when he walked in. Barney half expected a long-lost friend greeting. For three years he'd come in every second Tuesday, without fail, and invariably left a reasonable tip. Double at Christmas - not that he knew for sure if Ali celebrated Christmas. He came from Turkey, but that didn't mean Christian. Barney saw a feature about it once. The one time Ali grew a big bushy beard and people said he looked like a radical.

It had been three months since his last haircut, but Ali just nodded at the chair. Barney sat and described what he wanted. Ali nodded and turned on the clippers.

Barney over-tipped. The bag only contained fifty-dollar bills, and Ali said he couldn't make change. On the way home, he stopped for milk. Another fifty bucks. This time, they gave him change.

'Long time no see,' said the woman in the kosher bakery where he used to loiter for coffee. 'I figured you did a bunk.'

'No such luck,' Barney said with a smile. 'You won't lose me that easily.'

When she suggested a bagel, it didn't sound right to say no, so that's what Barney ate.

The next day, Barney took the subway downtown, he hung around outside the cop shop. His nerve didn't hold, instead he ducked into Whole Foods. It was strange putting things into his basket. Things he once bought without a second thought.

It came to more than he expected and the girl on the till acted weird when he offered her fifty bucks. She rolled her eyes and moaned to other customers about how pissed she was.

A guy begged outside. He had a lovely white dog with dark sad eyes.

'Cold today,' Barney said and dropped a ten-dollar bill in his hat.

The guy nodded.

Getting the power put back on proved a pain. He'd managed so long with candles. The woman he spoke to didn't sound like she had a heart.

'We'll need to fit a meter,' she said. 'It will recover your debt.'

The call ended with the promise she'd put a card in the mail for him to take to the shops and buy credit. They would fit the meter on Friday.

While buying credit, he bought a lottery ticket and won twenty bucks. Barney wondered if his luck had changed.

It had been a long time since Barney ate out. Taco Bell was hardly haute cuisine, but knowing there would be no plates to clean was a true luxury. He over-ordered and wrapped leftovers in a napkin, slipping it into his pocket for later. One thing they said about Barney. The guy planned ahead.

A woman with a pram bitched at the waiter, trying to use a coupon.

'It's out of date,' he kept saying.

'My kids are starving.'

'That's not my problem.'

Barney stepped in, and the first reaction was hostile.

'I don't want no charity.'

'I came into money. Something of a miracle. I simply wish to distribute my great fortune.'

She snatched the cash and hurled it at the guy on the till. Barney saw her later outside with a group of guys. They jeered when he waved.

Tonight was the first since Thursday when nobody came to his front door. And Barney felt miserable. They came with stories and he listened. The cash he gave them was payment due. He had no right to challenge their tales. He couldn't call anyone a phony.

Barney was a crook. A guy who found a sack of cash and kept it.

Eventually Maureen called. Word reached her about how her ex-husband was dressing smarter and buying bagels for guys begging on blankets. She'd heard he was dining at Taco Bell.

'I assume you have work again?'

'Yes,' he lied. 'They begged me to come back.'

'Well, don't try that on me.'

'Try what?'

'Don't beg *me* to come back.'

The thought had never crossed his mind. In his head, Maureen's chapter was closed.

'I miss having you around,' he said, more to be kind and help her save face than anything else.

'Fine,' she yelled. 'I'll get an Uber. You'll have to pay.'

He showed her the cash as they sipped champagne, and Maureen's eyes grew wide. Barney told her how wrong he felt about spending someone else's money, and how he'd tried to do good.

That night, when the guys came knocking, she answered the door. They asked where he was and she said he was out.

'Why do that?' Barney said.

Maureen shook her head. 'They take advantage. You're too friendly.'

He shrugged. 'Better I give them money than hold on to something I have no way of spending it.'

Maureen snorted. 'I can spend it. Don't you worry.'

She was counting it again when a brick sailed through the window. She slipped from her chair and her head made a strange crunching noise when she hit the floor. There was blood. Everywhere.

The ambulance guy pronounced her dead at the scene and Barney nodded.

* * *

'Why didn't you come in sooner?' said the cop when he stopped taking notes.

'You might assume I was to blame.'

'And the cash?'

Barney allowed the guy a smile. Maureen apart, he was the only other person to find out The first stranger he trusted. He stared as the cop piled it into a clear plastic bag.

'How much is there here?'

'When I last counted, ten grand, give or take. But I've given so much away.'

* * *

One judge ruled misadventure. Another convicted Barney of robbery. Everyone said he should have got a lawyer to argue his case. The local TV station had a phone-in.

'I'm better like this,' he said one morning when the prison doctor came to check his blood pressure. 'The days are much easier when you figure what to expect.'

The doctor peered at a screen. 'It's normal, you can go back to the others.'

* * *

They never had kids, and the only person at Barney's cremation was the woman from the kosher bakery. When she heard they discovered him hanging in a cell, she organised a collection to make sure the poor guy whose name he never got to know had a decent send off.

'You didn't have to kill him,' she told her husband on visiting day.

'That was my cash. I left it there for you.'

'All the same.'

As the pastor delivered words about someone, he didn't know, she whispered goodbye.

'You poor shit. I bet you figured out it was your lucky day.'

Lobster

'They say the lobster here is to die for,' Louise says and leans back in her chair.

Joe wants to pinch himself. Which lucky star sent her into his store to ask for directions?

Beautiful women deserve beautiful things. Chateau Bernard turned out to be a great idea.

'You order whatever you want, honey,' Joe says and hopes his voice stays even. Lobster isn't cheap.

Louise puts down her menu and clicks her fingers.

The waiter is busy serving steak tartar to a guy in a shiny suit.

'Hey Mohammed,' she says. 'Pull your finger out your ass and get over here.'

Joe rarely eats in fancy joints, but he's pretty sure this isn't the way to get great service. His brother waits tables down town and often tells stories of how kitchen staff spit in the soup of shitty customers.

He makes a mental note to stick with salad.

A different guy serves drinks. He pours a tiny trickle into Joe's glass. Joe waits and wills him to carry on.

'He wants you to sample the wine,' Louise says. 'Tell him it isn't like vinegar.'

Joe is no wine expert. He'd be happier with a beer, but this is Chateau Bernard. People here drink wine.

'It's cool,' he says, as the waiter fills their glasses.

Louise acts flirty, and it leaves Joe awkward.

The guy serving wine is tall and blonde, with blue eyes. The kid you wanted to be at school.

'Do you also take food orders?' she says. 'I'm so hungry.'

'Wine only ma'am. My colleague will assist you.'

She looks put out.

'Fine. But make sure Mohammed knows we don't got all evening.'

Joe's heart sinks a little. All evening is what he hoped they might have. And a little more. Tonight is their third date. Suggesting dinner took every ounce of his courage. Lunch would be cool, but dinner suggests cocktails, a nightcap. A shared cab home. Perhaps she'll invite him in for coffee.

Louise's mouth forms a grim line.

'What's wrong, honey?' he says.

'That nigger got served before us. I guess Mohammed likes to look after his own.'

The people at the next table pretend not to hear.

'The waiter is Asian,' Joe reasons. 'That guy is black.'

'Black, yellow, brown. They're all the same.'

She has lipstick on her teeth, and he ought to say something, but Joe is in awe of Louise.

Such a beautiful woman, and she's having dinner with him.

At Chateau Bernard.

Life doesn't get much better.

'I guess he saw I'm still choosing,' Joe says and puts down his menu. 'My fault.'

Louise looks around and Joe wills their eyes to meet. Making a connection is key. He read that in his mother's Cosmopolitan.

'Why didn't you make an effort?' she says. 'That suit looks old.'

'I came straight from work.'

'You didn't shower?'

'I don't sweat much. Nobody in our family does.'

Louise wrinkles her nose.

The other waiter comes back, and Louise acts like she doesn't notice.

'Honey,' Joe says. 'Are you ready to order?'

'I need more time.'

He nods and goes to get pretzels.

'Are they gluten-free?' she says.

'Why don't I ask?'

'I can't digest gluten. Gluten can kill me. My father is a lawyer. He'll shut you down.'

Joe smiles. You learn so much about people over dinner.

* * *

The meal starts with the most delicate of salads. Louise tells Joe about how she once ate the same dish in Paris, in a place where the house band played a song in her honor.

'I felt like the cat's meow,' she said. 'My date was a banker, he thought it all so gay.'

'Gay?'

'I hate how words get twisted. Such a pretty expression, corrupted by faggots.'

'We can't use that word, these days, Louise.'

She shakes her head.'Ho-mo-sex-u-al. Say what you like. Don't you consider it a pity so many beautiful words get stolen?'

Louise writes poetry. She fancies herself an intellectual. On their first date, they went to a gallery in town. Watercolors by a local artist. She talked him into buying one. Joe walked to work for the rest of the week.

When the plates clear, she orders more wine.

'But we didn't finish the first bottle.'

'You can't drink red wine with Lobster.'

'Right,' says Joe. 'I forgot.'

* * *

He often wondered how Lobster might taste. The one time in San Francisco he tried crab, but everyone always said Lobster was something else.

'It's good,' he says, but Louise pulls an angry face.

'Mohammed,' she cries. 'This Lobster is cold. It's stone fucking cold.'

Their waiter is busy laying a table, he looks over.

'Take mine,' Joe says. 'Mine is just about perfect. Maybe a little too hot. I like my food cooler. I should eat yours. You should eat mine. How about it?'

'Fuck you,' Louise says. 'I don't want food you already dribbled over.'

She demands to talk to the manager and a miserable guy promises to strike her main course from the bill and when he goes into the kitchen to berate their chef, Louise leans in to whisper.

'We'll get the wine free too. Dumb fucking A-rab.'

Desert is a swirl of berries around a wobbly cream jelly. Nothing to write home about.

'Panna cotta.' Louise closes her eyes as she speaks, like she's a million miles away. 'I once ate this in Venice.'

'That's Spain, right?'

She looks pissed. 'Italy, Joe. It's in Italy.'

She calls over the guy in charge of wine.

'What do you recommend we drink with dessert?' she says. 'A Sauternes?'

She catches him counting money under the table.

'Jesus, Joe,' she says. 'Don't act cheap.'

The wine arrives, and he takes a sip. It tastes like cough syrup.

After dinner, Louise orders Coffee with Amaretto and Joe excuses himself.

Alone at the table, Louise laughs. It's been a wonderful evening. She might even let this loser take her out again sometime. He'll expect a kiss. A fumble. She must let him trust that there's a future. Just like she does with the others.

Men. They're so pathetic.

The manager hands her a slip of paper, folded neat. He looks embarrassed.

'Your friend asked me to pass on this note. He had to leave.'

Anger bubbles. How dare anyone walk out on her? Especially that loser.

'Business,' she says. 'My friend runs a real estate company. With offices in London and Rome. They call him all the time.'

The manager nods and looks away. Is he laughing at her?

'Call me a cab,' she snaps. 'And make sure the driver is white.'

She pulls her shawl tight and shoves him to one side, but he takes a hold of her arm.

'About the bill…'

All at once she isn't so sure of an appropriate move. Did that jerk duck out without paying? She reaches into her pocket and has to put on glasses to make sense of Joe's childish scrawl.

His words make her gasp.

"Go fuck yourself. You're ugly inside."

* * *

Joe loves Max's Taphouse. It's like on that TV show. Everybody knows your name. For sure, he shouldn't be there. What he did to Louise was kind of shitty.

He's happy to see Max's niece Nancy working behind the bar.

'How did the big date go?' she says. 'You're here, so I'm guessing things didn't go to plan.'

'Could have been better.'

She laughs.

'Louise Bywater is a prick tease. I tried to warn you.'

She hands him a beer.

'This one is on the house. I guess dinner doesn't come cheap at Chateau Bernard.'

He settles at the bar, and across the way spies Ahmed. Every day that kid sits on the sidewalk and begs for money. Some days Joe stops to talk. Ahmed's mother is sick. She can't go out to work. Some days he doesn't eat.

'Save my place,' he tells Nancy. 'I have something to do.'

At closing time, Nancy wakes a drunk slumped at the bar.

'Time to hit the road, buddy.'

Joe gets his coat, but she stops him.

'One for the road?'

They drink whiskey. And not the watered down crap that Max serves. Nancy knows where to find the good stuff.

'I saw you with Ahmed.'

'The kid deserved a break.'

'Did someone die and leave you a million? Dinner at Chateau Bernard and still have enough left to give handouts to street kids.'

'I did something bad,' he says. 'I set out to make it right. Louise will never talk to me again.'

'Screw her. One of these days you can take me to dinner…'

He allows himself a smile. Did this mean the hottest girl in town was coming on to Joe McDonald?

Did a pig just fly by?

'Sure, Nancy. And tell you what. We'll have lobster.'

Barney

'We should get a dog,' she said and Mike looked up from his book. She sat in front of the mirror, her eyes closed, like she was some place else, probably with someone else.

'Really, honey?' he said. 'You know I have allergies.'

'It would be wonderful,' she said as if she didn't hear.

Mike doubted this use of wonderful.

Getting a dog would mean the end of sunshine vacations. There could be no last-minute weekends driving through the desert. They might as well cancel their account at Bath and Beyond. And as for having nice clothes. Forget it.

'We could take a dog for walks,' she said.

Mike wondered what kind of dog she had in mind.

Catherine didn't strike him as the sort to want a purse dog, she'd probably want a lab, or a lurcher. That was at least some consolation. A dog you could take out to bars, one that would sit at your feet and attract smiles from fellow drinkers.

He could talk to the pharmacist. There were tablets to deal with allergies.

'Fine,' he said. 'Let's look.'

She took him at his word, and the next morning they went to the shelter. Mike hated every dog he saw even though he had to make faces that suggested otherwise. They were all too old, barked too much, acted kinda nervous, didn't have friendly eyes.

'We could buy a dog,' he said when drove away.

Catherine looked wounded.

'These little guys need us.'

'They need *someone*,' he said carefully. 'They don't specifically need us. You saw how busy that place was. All those kids who would love a dog.'

He glanced over, her expression was blank.

'I read something in the Chronicle about puppy farms. Those guys suffer too. We'd still be helping. It would be a different rescue.'

She nodded but stayed silent. Mike didn't quit and by the time they parked up, he'd won her over.

'What sort of dog,' she said as she logged onto the computer

'Medium size.'

She typed something in.

'Jack Russell?'

'That would be cool,' Mike said. 'Like Eddie in Frasier.'

Catherine looked blank.

'It's a good thing,' he said. 'They have personality.'

She started to read.

'Maybe not, honey. It says here they like to dig.'

'How is that a problem? We don't have a garden.'

'Exactly. How awful would it be if we take a dog that wants to dig and put him in a third-floor apartment?'

Mike nodded agreement even though he wondered if she might be talking nonsense.

They dismissed Airedales for having a temper around other dogs. Research proved that basset hounds were stubborn.

'A bulldog,' Mike said hopefully. 'A British Bulldog.'

He would picture himself in the park with his new best friend.

'They snore,' she said.

'So do you.'

'I don't.' She looked appalled. 'Do I?'

'Only occasionally and it's cute.'

Why mention he relied on industrial strength earplugs most nights, hidden in the bedside table, slipped in when she taxied down the runway and roared into flight.

'They're no good in tropical climates,' she said.
'So that's perfect.'
'Remember last summer, when the air-co broke down?'
'For about an hour.'
She shook her head and carried on looking.

***

Mike was at the office when Catherine called. Her voice was full of excitement.
'Don't be mad at me.'
'OK.' He put on his most upbeat voice.
'I found us a dog.'
In all honesty Mike imagined the whole dog thing to have blown over and had been waiting for her next impulse buy. He'd caught her looking at a website offered shared ownership of beach front condos the previous evening.
'You'll love him,' she said. 'Just try not to slam any doors when you get home. He's still nervous.'
When Mike thought about it over a brown bag lunch, he wasn't actually that annoyed that she'd found a dog without him. He'd done his by best to help, but it was like everything else. His role was to nod and agree.

***

Barney was a strange creature. An oversize bundle of wiry black hair, saliva and crazy white eyes. He'd launch himself at your legs every time you entered a room, making the hee-haw noises you'd expect from an asthmatic donkey.
But Mike loved Barney and Barney loved Mike.
'You two are inseparable,' Catherine said. 'I ought to be jealous.'
Mike laughed…
'You're not though?'
'No, of course not. What kind of crazy bitch would that make me?'

BARNEY

He knew this to be a lie. She was very jealous.

***

'He's ruined my shoes,' she said and held up what looked like a piece of Impressionist sculpture. If it was once a shoe, her choice of the word ruined was perfect.

'He's just settling in. It's probably anxiety.'

'Oh, so suddenly you're the dog whisperer.'

'Dogs chew things, it's what they do. You knew this when we got him.'

He saw how Catherine bit her lower lip. Barney needed to do something big to win her back over.

'I'm going for a walk with him. Why don't you come? We can throw sticks. He's brilliant when he can't find the right one.'

'I'm not in the mood.'

'You never are.'

He meant nothing by it, but boy did she take offense.

'He's your fucking dog. You walk him.'

She went into the kitchen, and he heard the ruined shoes go into the trash.

Barney looked up from licking his lower half.

Mike grinned.

'Now we're both in the doghouse, he said. Time to make ourselves scarce.'

***

Everyone in his local bar loved Barney. Mary who managed the place used to feed him salami. It gave him ferocious wind, and Catherine hated that. Mike found it hilarious.

***

'It isn't fair on Barney to be left on his own all day,' she said one evening as she sat at the dressing table.

'He's fine.'

'He might act fine, but it isn't right. I'm sure the neighbors think we're mistreating him.'

'Screw them. Why would you care?'

'Maybe we need to rethink things.'

'We could pay a dog walker.'

'Have you seen how much they charge? We could go on vacation to Cuba for less.'

Mike knew the specific nature of her reply suggested she had done her research.

'Maybe I'll work from home more.'

'What message does that send out to everyone in your team?'

'People with kids do it all the time.'

'Barney isn't a child,' she said and her voice quivered.

Mike knew at once what the problem was.

Catherine lay on the floor, her head next to his. Their breathing fell into step.

'They could be wrong,' she said.

'Maybe.'

'We'll manage fine on our own.'

I guess.

Mike was shocked by the feeling of grief that overwhelmed him when the test results finally came.

'Lots of people get by without kids,' she said.

'I know.'

There was a scratching at the door

'I guess he wants to come in,' Mike said. 'He senses something.'

She looked up, and despite everything a smile took over.

Barney treated them to meaty kisses, did the hee-haw and pushed his way between them. Catherine's arms went around him and Mike saw how happy that made them both.

There may never be kids, but they had the next best thing.

Barney broke wind, and the room filled with the putrid stench of burning

BARNEY

tires.

'It's your turn to take him out,' Mike said.

She hugged the dog tighter, and his eyes closed.

Mike joined the circle.

'In a while,' she said.

The game is over

Oscar Daily killed out there. The audience loved him. Back on form, and back at the top of his game. In the dressing room, he waits. Fans will come and beg for an autograph, just like they always do. There will be those who hang around with a special smile, like they expect something more. Groupies they used to call them. He won't leave this crap-hole alone. That's for sure.

There's a note stuck to the cracked mirror to say Ed Moran called. Isn't that a turn up for the book? After all these years, Eddie Boy wants to talk. Maybe they can revive the double act. Perhaps a state tour. If all those boy bands and has-beens can rise again, why not Daily and Moran? Goodbye to faceless dive bars and shitty clubs.

Someone knocks at the door. Oscar checks the mirror, wipes his face and runs a hand through thinning hair. 'Come in.'

It's a pretty girl with long blonde hair. Young and grinning like a loon. Devoid of sophistication. The sort you get in rust belt.

'You looking for me, sweet-pea?' he says.

She nods though her eyes stay fixed to the floor.

'Well, don't hang around like a terrible smell. Shut the door you're letting in the night.'

It clicks shut.

'Well ain't you a pretty little thing?'

She doesn't reply.

'You fancy a drink?'

She shakes her head.

'You won't mind if I do, though, eh?'

He pulls a bottle from his bag. It's already half empty.

'You sure I can't tempt you?'

Two slugs later, and she still gives him the silent treatment. Why the fuck did she bother coming in here?

'Is it an autograph you're after?' he says, deciding that maybe tonight he will get to leave the place alone. He looks closer. 'Jesus, how old are you?'

What if someone came in and found him here with this child?

'You got an autograph book or something?' he says. 'I'm all out of pictures, waiting for new ones from the printers.'

Still she doesn't answer.

'Your folks will wonder where you got to. I have to get back to my motel room.'

He goes to take another slug of brandy, but stops when he sees she's crying. This is all he needs.

Oscar puts down the bottle. 'There now, sweet-pea, what's up with your heart?'

He goes to put an arm around her shoulder, but she runs for the door, only looking up as it opens. That's when he recognizes the eyes.

'Jacqueline?'

* * *

Oliver punches in a once familiar number. The first few times he gets it wrong and has to apologize to a woman who says she'll phone the cops if he does it again.

'Eddie Boy, long time no see,' he says when it answers.

Static crackles cause the faraway voice to distort. This crappy cell bought off a guy in a bar has never worked.

'I got your message.'

The line clicks, there's nobody there.

The theater manager will be round soon to chuck him out. It's hard to believe nobody came backstage. Apart from that kid. He did a good show. People laughed. Like they used to. He'll call his agent tomorrow and give a report. It won't be long before the press talks about the comeback kid.

That girl was creepy. The way her eyes reminded him of Jacqueline. He went to her funeral, said his piece. Shook hands with the family. They thanked him for stepping in and paying for the flowers.

Saint Oscar, they called him. The nation's favorite uncle.

There's another knock at the door.

Finally!

This is more like it. Curly red hair, too much lipstick, tight top, little denim jacket and nice long legs.

'Hey there.'

He stands to let her sit, and she studies his face, with no hint of a smile. Like someone looking at dog shit on good shoes. Again, it's the eyes that give her away.

'Mary,' he says. 'What the... How?'

She shakes her head.

'It can't be. Who the hell are you, anyway? They never said she had a sister. Is that it? You're Jackie's sister?'

The door closes, and she's gone. Alone in the stinking room, Oscar's hands shake as he finishes the brandy. It's nearly 11.30. He better get his jacket and leave.

The stench of overflowing bins fills the alley. No fans hang around for autographs. Not like the old days. He heads towards the main street and flashing lights. Cops, no doubt. Drunken kids fighting.

'Uncle Oscar.' The voice makes him jump. It belongs to a woman in a gray mac. She's old, but beggars can't be choosers.

'All right, sweet-pea?' he says. 'You saw the show tonight?'

'You killed them,' she says.

At last! Someone with a kind word to say. He *knew* he'd nailed it.

'I wasn't half bad, was I? You don't fancy heading to a bar for a nightcap?'

She links an arm through his, and they totter towards the flashing lights. He recognizes her perfume. One he hasn't smelled in years. Didn't even know they still made it.

THE GAME IS OVER

She stops, and this causes him to stumble.

'You don't recognize me, do you?' she says.

It isn't only the perfume that's so familiar, it's the way she walks, the click of her heels. The lazy eye. The pouty bottom lip.

'How did you find me?' he says.

'I came looking. You *knew* I would.'

He stumbles towards the flashing lights and the sound of walkie-talkies. A small crowd has gathered and two men in uniform wheel out a stretcher.

'What's happened?' he says, but nobody replies.

'I suppose they'll never know,' says the man next to him.

'Know what?'

A woman shakes her head.

'Those poor kids. The bastard escaped justice by the steam on his shit. They should have thrown away the key.'

Oscar tries again. 'What's happened?'

They carry on their conversation as if he wasn't there.

'Did you see Eddie Moran on the news? Claims he knew nothing about it. They worked together for years. How come he suspected nothing? You can't go messing with kids and have nobody know.'

The ambulance doors close. Someone throws a bottle, and it smashes on the ground.

'You knew they'd find out one day.'

That voice again. He turns to see two figures.

'What's going on?'

Those eyes. He knows those eyes.

'Jennifer?'

She nods.

'Mary?'

The two women link arms and walk away. The theater shutters clatter down. The crowd moves away and Oscar gets it. He isn't here any longer.

The game is up.

The game is over.

Nothing like February

Amanda waits by the road, under a streetlight so he'll notice her when he comes, driving his sensible car that tells the outside world he's a steady guy. Some may call her foolish to wait alone in the depth of night, but they don't understand what all of this means.

He didn't establish a time. She asked twice, but all he'd do was smile.
Tonight. Sometime.
After all these years, it felt like enough, and she taunted herself to ask if she could inform the others. He said no.
And he was right, they wouldn't understand.
So, she kept it from Amelia even though the flowers she brought that morning smelled so delicious. She kept the truth from Josh when he showed up to read her another of his tragic poems. She kept it from the twins - who, let's be fair, only ever called round to gawk at Josh. She laughed to herself when they swooned and announced someone should publish his work. The guy can't write for toffee. Are they deaf?
She paused at the window and decided the night looked cold. After so many stormy days, snow was on the way. Amanda unwrapped her mother's mink stole. It never crossed her mind she might one day wear it. The twins had done her face. Badly.
So what? It was dark. Who would care?
When she stepped outside, the evening air felt mellow. Nothing like February.

Amanda looks at her wristwatch. Three o'clock. This is what they call the dead of night. An appropriate time for their reunion.

That morning, Chloe appeared on her doorstep. They kissed and hugged, neither choosing to ask why it had taken so long. Amanda let Chloe follow her into the living room. She sprawled on the sofa and tuned in to what should have been a confession. This friendly visit came with a purpose.

'I was as stunned as anyone when he produced the ring,' Chloe twittered.

Amanda laughed and said how *charming* it looked. The twins proclaimed themselves *blown away*.

When the hour was correct to take her leave, Chloe sounded anything but humble. 'We've left matters too long.'

'None of this came as my decision.'

'We should never have let it develop. You realize that now?'

Charles showed himself a weak man. The bitch was welcome to him.

Sounds from the garden cause Amanda's head to swivel. A fox, maybe rats. Maria never secures the garbage sacks. Is it any wonder that every hungry creature comes to feast?

Three days ago, Amanda paid a last visit to the peninsula. Her guide spoke of how the summer would bring color and the designs he had for different planting patterns. The geese flew skyward. Home early. And who can blame them? It's nothing like February. When the snow swirls in on the east side, they'll perish too. How she wanted to wave them away.

Everyone made it clear when she eventually agreed to leave the peninsula that the visits must cease. She only wept when alone. To let anybody see would cause false hope.

Four fifteen and still no sign. Soon it will become light as the early morning people rise. The mailman, the factory workers, guys who tend to gardens.

Charles was so sure of himself. Certain she didn't know about the games he enjoyed when left alone with Chloe. He played the part of the doting husband when anybody called. He spoke the right words, talking of medical science and miracles, kissing her so tenderly that Amanda sometimes wondered if she'd got everything wrong.

Even on the day she snapped and packed her bag, he protested that she'd got it all wrong. As Amanda lingered in the hall, waiting for a taxi driver, he fussed around, acting like she was leaving for the most wonderful vacation.

'You'll have such a marvelous time at the lake house, Amanda. We need this space to think and sort out what was said. To forgive.'

It was as if he believed her words to be little more than a flicker of rage.

If only she hadn't seen.

Thinking something was wrong caused pain. Knowing it hurt like hell.

A car slows down. The driver craning to find out who squats on the sidewalk, with all that matters in a clear plastic Ziploc. Her glasses. Her wedding ring. The necklace she won at the county fair. Worth nothing. She waits for more headlights to brighten pale gray skies.

The upstairs lights burned brightly at Josh's place. A tortured artist starved of dreams. He'd looked stunned when she knocked upon the door.

'It's late. Are you OK?'

Surely anyone could see she wasn't.

'May I come in?'

He let her sleep on his sofa, lending a cashmere blanket, perfumed with lavender.

What will he imagine has happened when he finds her gone?

Amanda gets to her feet, so sure a car parked further down the block must be the one. She dares herself to look back and startles at his face. How long was he watching?

'Darling?' Charles says. 'Come back inside.'

She let herself into the house and snaked up the stairs, slipping the mink stole into its hiding place.

'The doctor will be here soon,' Charles said and nodded at the bed. Amanda forced a smile.

He whispered to Maria from the other side of the bedroom door. 'My wife is sleeping. Please keep the children busy.'

Soon comes the sizzle of bacon. The sun shines and birds sing. It's nothing like February.

Hemmingway

For sale.
Wedding ring.
Bought in error.

The Armchair Bride

The path to true love starts with drunken new year resolutions... and the smallest of white lies.

With her fortieth birthday looming, Lisa Doyle wonders where things went wrong. Everyone from school is married with kids - or living better lives. And she should know. She's got cyberstalking down to a fine art.

Tired of feeling the odd one out, Lisa updates her online profile, adding a husband. An astronaut in training who saves lives. It's no big deal. Everyone lies online.

If only Helen could have announced her shotgun wedding sooner. And not begged Lisa to organise a hen night... for all those friends from school simply dying to meet her fabulous new husband.

Does she brazen it out, or come clean?

It sets the scene for a year in the life of an armchair bride.

The Armchair Bride was published by Spring Street Books and is available through all online bookstores and - if you hunt hard enough - in actual shops.

ISBN-10: 0955988535 | **ISBN-13:** 978-0955988530

Chapter One

Ten, nine, eight...
Does anyone love New Year's Eve? If I had my way, I'd be in bed with a good book and a huge glass of wine. Not stuck to a threadbare carpet in a Manchester theatre function room and forced to pretend I want to spend the dying hours of the year with the same people I see every working day.
Seven, six ...
Someone grabs my hand and drags me to the dance-floor. They tell me to "cheer up, it might never happen" and I play along, faking the most cheesy grin.
Might never happen? I think it already has.
Five, four, three...
We link arms, and the anticipation grows. A new year, new hopes, new dreams. On the stroke of midnight, lives will change.
Two... one...
The room erupts as Big Ben chimes and bagpipes quail. Streamers pop and party people hug, kiss and stumble.
Should old acquaintance be forgot and never brought to mind...
I mouth the first few words, air-kiss colleagues and do my absolute best to act like I'm having oodles of fun. Across the room, my flatmate mine-sweeps abandoned glasses, necking leftover wine. My boss does the rounds, shaking hands, exchanging words. As gestures go, it's way too formal in a room where forgotten faces grin down from dog-eared pantomime posters.
I've worked with Brian for nine years, and although it's never come up, I'm sure we're about the same age. Our cultural references tally and we exchange looks of dread when younger people use words like totes, bear or sick. I suppose he's good

looking in a greying-at-the-temples soccer dad way, and he keeps himself in shape. Brian dresses well and happens to have perfect teeth. Mam would call him *a decent catch*. The stumbler here being he's married. To Audrey. Who everyone at the Empire Theatre fears.

Because she *is* terrifying.

'Am I getting a kiss?' I say when it gets to be my turn.

Brian looks around before he leans in to land the slightest peck.

'Happy new year, Lisa. Are you here with Andy?'

I nod and reheat my best fake smile. Of course I'm with Andy. I'm *always* with Andy. There's a running joke about how we come as a pair.

Brian grins. 'Someone told me you came with a boyfriend, and I said I was sure you were still single.'

He means nothing by it, and would be mortified to know how much a throwaway comment hurts.

I throw back my head and laugh.

'You know me Brian. Young, free and single. Only not so much of the young. Sisters are doing it for themselves.'

I've no idea why I sound like a perimenopausal Spice Girl.

'Right … so … that's good.' He takes a subtle step back from the crazy lady.

'Happy new year, boss,' I say and stifle an urge to salute.

Brian flicks a nervous glance. 'I best get back to Audrey.'

Ten minutes after midnight on New Year's Eve is the worst time ever to give yourself a *'where did it all go wrong?'* pep talk. With my left foot jammed against a graffitied toilet door, I wish myself away. Twelve months ago - to the night - I insisted much the same. My lifestyle shopping list was short: boyfriend, promotion, fit into (what I'm sure are wrongly labelled) jeans.

I'm still single, still doing the same job and, on Christmas Eve, found the inner strength to hide the jeans in a bin bag of cast-offs dumped in the doorway of a cat rescue shop.

That's not to say I'm unhappy. Why would I be? Who needs a boyfriend when I share my life with Andy? We've been best mates for close on 20 years and made a pledge long ago to never become *sad normals*. Like anyone who's been around the block and feared for a lonely old age, we've agreed a marriage pact. If single 40 ever rolls over to solo 60, we'll wave the white flag and do what every other loser does. Fake a happy union to save on heating costs. Until then, we're fine on our own.

People still talk about us as a pair.

Invite Andy and Lisa.

Will Andy and Lisa be there?

The flat share thing renders us socially acceptable and allows us a taste of coupledom. Without the need to find reasons not to have sex. I still get to watch what I want on Netflix and don't have to make out like I care about his boring mates. Best of all, I get to inhale a family size bar of Dairy Milk without guilt.

I date. Though rarely expecting success.

My brief encounters with suitable men come courtesy of blind dates engineered by well-meaning friends. I tried Tinder once. It ended badly with me seeking legal advice to slap a restraining order on a man called Tom who sent me daily tokens of his love. Locks of his ex-wife's hair, shards of her wedding dress, a photo of them together with my face superglued on hers.

And he proved to be one of my more successful dates.

New Year's Eve is when the nagging doubts grow loud. What if the sad normals actually have it right?

Mam insists there's an old shoe for every old sock, and a quick search online throws up photos of the much better times that *everyone* I ever knew at school looks to be having. Dinner parties in Farrow & Ball homes, designer-frocked cocktail receptions in chi-chi bars. The girls I assumed would end up in prison pose happily with a Subaru, labradoodle and scrubbed-up children.

And here's me, in the staff loo, alone.

Mam is right to worry. I'm the middle child and each time I find myself ditched, she says the same thing:

'What did you do to scare this one off, Lisa? We were *all* convinced he'd be the one.'

By *all*, she means my two sisters, and their lovely husbands. She also means all of her neighbours, our priest, sixteen of her closest friends and anyone with time to listen in the post office. By all accounts, Mrs Gupta, who handles the QVC returns, considers it an *absolute scandal* I'm not yet spoken for.

CHAPTER ONE

She suggested burning herbs and lighting special candles to turn everything around.

I've become a stranger's pet project.

'Lisa. Don't take this the wrong way, but if you want to come out of the cupboard, it's fine with all of us,' Mam said when I called to check she'd got my Christmas cards.

'I have no idea what you're talking about.'

'Your father loved Virginia Wade and that Clair Balding is always nicely turned out. I was thinking of buying myself a pair of jodhpurs.'

The penny landed with a crash.

'I'm not gay, Mam.'

'You're in denial.'

'Andy is gay. I'm straight.'

'They can marry these days. I saw it on Coronation Street. Not that it ended well for the two lasses there. One of them nearly chucked herself off the underwear factory roof, but the wedding itself was lovely. I've always thought you might suit lemon.'

I changed the subject. Mam never means to sound like she froths at the mouth. Mostly, I blame the Daily Mail and the fact that my sisters like to wind her up. She has my best intentions at heart.

For years, she liked to send pages torn from local newspapers showing former classmates dressed in horrible frocks and posing with new husbands.

'If fat Leslie Walker can snare a chap, you can too, Lisa.'

I blame her for *'The Spreadsheet'*.

Through the magic of Excel, I keep track of *every* girl from school. Each wedding, birth, messy split and second marriage gets recorded. It makes for depressing reading. The girls from class 5B at Erdington Comp are pretty much all spoken for; except for me and my onetime bestie Helen. But lately she's been seeing someone, and her last email humble bragged about trips to garden centres, so it's only a matter of time before she issues *save the date* cards.

Another impatient party-goer hammers on the toilet door.

'Hurry up. There's a queue.'

Back in the land of pretending to have the best time ever, Andy tracks me down.

'How much longer do we need to endure this hellhole?'

I'm about to suggest an escape plan when a booming voice calls my name and chills my heart.

'Audrey,' I say, and try not to look terrified. Brian's wife is far from my biggest fan. She blames me for the state he ended up in after a tequila-fuelled cast and crew party in July.

She isn't wrong.

'Have you seen my husband?' she says. 'Reliable sources suggest he was last spotted with you.'

'He was kissing everyone,' I say too quickly. 'And it wasn't only me.'

Her face turns to stone, and I look to Andy for help.

'Fabulous party,' he says. 'How do you manage it year after year?'

Disarmed, she fans herself with podgy fingers. 'One does one's best.'

It's like she doesn't see the scattered debris, the spent Prosecco corks, torn tatty streamers and paper plates of abandoned beige food.

'Shouldn't you mingle?' she says with a sniff. 'You're junior management. We pay for occasions like these to facilitate team bonding.'

Half an hour of forced smiles leaves my jaw numb. I need to find Andy and scarper. Except I suspect that's what he's already done. Most likely to some crowded gay bar to have a much better time.

Defeated, I seek a chair in the darkest corner. A place to hide until it's safe to leave without causing upset. Automatic impulse sends me back online to read friend updates. A soft-focus, high-filter gallery from a spiteful girl who made my young life hell. Like all the *sad normals*, Ginny Baker is having fun; grinning for the camera on the arm of some bloke at what looks like a Hollywood-themed party. Ginny doesn't know I stalk her. Her security settings are shot.

A text pings from Helen to wish me a happy new year, and I imagine her at a brilliant party, with brilliant friends, having a brilliant time.

I reply with a sad face selfie and tell her I'm at a theatre party.

She texts back "jel-jel" and I reply "lol".

CHAPTER ONE

We like to crack on we're down with the kids.

Over by the bar, Brian raises a glass and mouths *do you want a drink?*

I hold my nose and pull a face. He laughs, but still heads over.

'I got you one anyway,' he says. 'They tell me after six you stop noticing how awful it is.'

'The wine or this party?'

He looks around, his eyes wide. 'Both.'

'Don't let Audrey hear you say that.'

'She's too busy sucking up to the trustees to care what I think. She's made it her mission to have the Royal Box refurbished.'

'If that happens, where will I go to eat my lunch?'

'Where will *I* hide to do the crossword?'

He pulls out a chair, sits and catches sight of Ginny's photos on my phone. 'Friend of yours?'

'We went to school together.'

'Really? She looks a lot older.'

I treat him to a rare genuine smile. 'Just for that I won't bug you for a wage rise in January.'

A girl from accounts stumbles past with a bunch of mistletoe. We fake earnest conversation until the coast is clear.

'Good move,' Brian says, and I laugh. When he dares to loosen up, he's brilliant company.

'How's your evening been?' I say.

'Totes sick.'

Audrey hovers near the DJ booth, arms folded, glaring in our direction.

'Don't look now,' I say. 'We're getting the death stare.'

He doesn't move his lips as he speaks. 'Is it Audrey?'

I nod.

'Fine,' he says and gets to his feet. 'I'll throw myself on her mercy and take one for the team.'

For such a nice guy, he lacks any hint of a spine.

I watch her jab him with a podgy finger and issue orders. He looks around helpless. Poor guy.

I'm lost in another online loop when Andy appears.

'I thought you left,' I say.

'Get your coat. We're going to the Mineshaft.'

'Isn't it men only?'

'Keep your head down, nobody will know the difference.'

'If it's all the same to you…'

He grabs my hand. Resistance is futile.

The drink hits as we step outside and I find myself frog-marched to a waiting taxi. The gum-chewing cab driver peers over his shoulder as I collapse in a heap on his back seat. 'Is your lady going to be sick?'

Outraged, I try to point out I'm not anybody's *lady*, but the words come out slurred, and Andy takes over.

'The contents of my lady's stomach will be the least of your problems if you don't get us to the Mineshaft within the next ten minutes.'

In slow-moving traffic, drunks hammer on the cab windows.

'Is this the fastest you can go?' Andy says.

'New Year's Eve, mate. You'd be quicker walking.'

'Just drive. Run them over if need be.' When he pokes a finger in my ribs, I squeal. 'Don't fall asleep on me, Lisa. It's still early.'

'I've had enough. I want to go home.'

The driver's eyes lock onto mine. 'Are you OK, miss? This lad's not bothering you?'

'Oh please,' Andy snaps. 'The last man that bothered her lost the use of an eye. Your concern is noted, but do what you're being paid to do and drive.'

'I'm fine,' I say. 'This is how we talk to each other.'

Andy's arm slips around my shoulder, and he pulls me close. 'That staff party *was* awful. Why can't straights ever get it right? We need to find better excuses next year.'

'Brian hated it too.'

He nods, but says nothing.

'Audrey forced him to come.'

'Yeah, whatever…'

'He's actually OK, you know?'

CHAPTER ONE

Andy shifts in his seat to face me. 'If he's so fabulous, why don't you have an affair?'

My cheeks burn. 'Andy …'

He throws back his head and howls. 'Jesus, Lisa. Your face. I was taking the piss. If Audrey got wind of you lusting about dreamy Brian she'd break both your legs with a lump hammer.'

We join a line of cars at red lights.

'This is insane,' he says. 'We'll do our resolutions now.'

Each year, Andy and I pledge something mad that we know will never happen just for the hell of it. It's become our thing. Twelve months back I said I would pilot a plane and learn salsa. He pledged fluency in French.

'New rule this year, we have to choose for each other,' he says and I blink slowly in confusion. 'Just make something up … like tell me I have to have sex with more than three men called Dave.'

'Do you *know* more than three men called Dave?'

'No, but that doesn't matter. Hurry. Tell me what my fabulous future holds.'

'I'm too drunk. Ask me in the morning.'

'It has to be tonight, or it won't count.'

'Fine.' I haul myself upright. 'You have to … be famous by this time next year.'

Andy's lips purse. I've broken one of our friendship rules. We *never* mention his less-than-stellar acting career. In common with most people in the Empire Theatre box office, he dreams of a life on the stage. To date, he's been a community theatre caterpillar and played a guy with bad breath in a telly commercial only aired on the Isle of Wight.

'Call your agent,' I say. 'Demand she put you up for more stuff. In fact, give me your phone. I'll do it.'

He slaps away my hand. 'That's not how show business works.'

'You're fantastic though,' I say. 'You can totally do it.'

Compliments always work with Andy.

'How are you defining … famous?'

'You get to appear on *The One Show*.'

'I already did.'

'Face in the crowd doesn't count. Full Matt Baker or nothing. Your turn, do me.'

I can tell from how his eyes narrow I won't like whatever vengeful thought has crossed his mind.

But it's New Year's Eve. Whatever we say will be forgotten in days.

'Right,' he says. 'You *really* want to do this?'

'You started it.'

'By this time next year, you need to find a husband.'

All at once, the fun is sucked away.

'That's not fair,' I whisper. 'Why not lose weight or stop eating leftovers from the bin?'

'Both would help make you more appealing to the opposite sex.'

'Think of something else.'

'I'm serious, Lisa. You spend half your life telling me how everyone you ever knew is married or paired off. Now it's your turn.'

Anger bubbles. Why is he even doing this? He knows how easily I bruise.

'Stop sulking,' he says. 'We'll hang around Strangeways on release day.'

'I *could* get a man, if I wanted one.'

He snorts and turns to gaze out of the window. 'Look at the state of that lass over there. She's trashed.'

'I could,' I persist. 'Maybe … I like being on my own.'

'Yeah, right. Whatever.'

'Fine,' I say. 'I accept your silly challenge. I will find myself a serious boyfriend.' Andy reaches for my hand, but I snatch it away. 'And call Beryl. Just for once let's do something with our lives.'

'Oh, come on, pumpkin,' he says. 'Don't let's fall out. Not tonight of all nights.'

Blood pumps in my ears, and my chest aches. I'm either having a heart attack or tasting true fear.

An idea forms. Before I can stamp it down, it takes hold.

'You're fired,' I say in my best Lord Sugar voice.

Andy cocks his head to one side. 'I'm what?'

'You heard me. I'm your manager, and you are now officially out of a job.

You're free to follow your dreams.'

'You can't fire me.'

'I just did.'

'On what grounds?'

'Insubordination.'

'Fuck off.'

'How about arguing with customers? What about that woman with the fur coat you threatened to napalm?'

'She had it coming. Fur's for fools.'

'Don't you see?' I say, warming to my subject. 'If you don't have to drag yourself into work each day, you'll get to focus on your calling.'

'My what?'

'Your calling. The roar of the crowd. The smell of the greasepaint.'

'Have you had a stroke?'

'You expect me to find a man. Surely *you* can manage to have someone recognise your talent. Go to Hollywood, hang around the studios. It's what you always said you'd do.'

'Hollywood?'

'London then. I'll pay your train fare.'

If Andy's having problems believing what he hears, he isn't the only one. I've no idea what spirit has hold, but I can't stop. Somehow, in this moment, it feels right.

'I'm letting you go,' I say. 'This way, it gives you the time and space to live your dream.'

'I'll report you to the union.'

'You've *always* hated working in the box office. You said yourself you'd leave if you could afford to. This is my gift to you. I can manage the rent for a month or two, and you get to concentrate on acting. Call it a sabbatical.'

'This is ridiculous.'

I take hold of his hand. 'If it doesn't work out, you can come back.'

We've reached the club. A queue of guys in leather chaps and gimp suits glare over as Andy springs from the cab and jumps the line. Our driver turns around.

'I'll marry you, love. What are you like with a chipper?'

I rummage in my bag for money. 'Do you have a business card? And keep every Saturday free next December. I might be in touch.'

The gift exchange

I've occasionally been asked what became of Lisa Doyle, the central character from The Armchair Bride. So here's a short story for Christmas to bring you up to date on her life these days. Two years on from the end of that book, Lisa's home with Brian for a family Christmas and about to run into a ghost from the past!

Mam looks up from the heap of Christmas cards gathered on the kitchen table.

'Do you have an address for Ginny Baker?' she says. 'Last thing I gathered, she was living in one of those new flats near the precinct.'

'You're not seriously sending her a card?' I say and try to hold my voice even. 'After all she did.'

'It's a time to forgive.'

'She almost got me killed.'

Mam shakes her head. 'It was a toy gun.'

'Nobody knew that.'

'Guru Westwood says you have to forgive to move on.' Mam scribbles a greeting in the card. 'Life's too short to carry grudges.'

Two months ago, Mam saw a flyer in the library for The Golden Buddha Trust–a group for retired people in search of answers to life's many questions. These days she loves everyone–except for Muriel opposite who never puts the lid on her recycling bin.

Brian dumps the oversize bag I insisted he pack in the hall.

'Do you need anything else from the car?' he says. 'I've left Amy and Sue's presents in the boot like you said.'

Mum rolls her eyes. 'What's wrong with putting gifts under the tree?'

'They'll keep prodding at them. Let's have surprises this year.'

Both Mam and Brian stare at my belly. My huge, eight-month pregnant belly.

'I think I've already had my share of surprises,' she says. 'Haven't there been enough secrets in this family?'

* * *

I found out I was expecting Lucinda on my forty-second birthday. Brian held my hand as a nurse smeared gel over my distended stomach, and we stared at the monitor to make sense of random light patterns.

'Do you want to know the sex?' the nurse asked and before Brian could answer I said yes.

The name came two days later.

'I read somewhere that the first name you think of is the right one and that you should write it down,' I said and offered a scrap of paper from my pocket.

On it, I'd written Lucinda.

Brian peered at it. 'When did you do that?'

My plan had been to act all mystical and maintain the name materialised in a dream, whispered by celestial voices. In fact, Lucinda was my Nan's name and Dad once made me promise to consider it if grandchildren came along.

'It's been in my head a while,' I said.

'Lucinda?' Brian made the name sound like one he'd never heard before. 'It's cute. Lucy for short.'

I relished the smug feeling of someone who knew best. Lucinda was a noble name; one not open for teasing.

* * *

The doorbell rings and Brian is sent to answer. There are voices and then a scratching at the door. Bertie pushes his nose round and dives into the bags gathered round my feet.

'Does this dog ever stop?' I cry as Mam laughs.

'Give him a biscuit,' she says. 'He loves digestives.'

The mere mention of the word biscuit has Bertie on his haunches, brown eyes blazing into mine.

My sister drags two reluctant offspring into the kitchen.

'Isn't Amy here yet?' she says, and everyone exchanges awkward looks.

'Glen has business to tend to,' Mam mutters darkly. 'Special business.'

Sue gets it at once, and even though her face flushes, she manages a smile.

* * *

Most families would applaud charity work. That one of their kin wants to give up time to hand out gifts to orphans and the homeless should be a good thing. And perhaps Mam would be on board with this had Glen agreed to camouflage himself as Santa Claus or even as an elf. It's his insistence on dressing as Susan Boyle that has her on edge.

'What time is it over?' Mam says.

'Amy reckoned they'll be here by five,' I say and look anxiously around. All I want to do is change the subject before she launches into another distinctly unforgiving, un-Buddhist rant. I'm too late.

'Don't get me wrong. I've tried to understand,' she says. 'But it has me perplexed. I constantly wonder if I'd have been happier if he had been having a liaison. A father who gets his jollies by putting on women's knickers? Well, it's not the ideal environment for a child.'

'How can you say that?' Sue jumps in to defend Glen and Amy. 'Tishiba is the happiest little girl living.'

'There's that name again,' Mam says. 'It sounds like someone should stand her in Dixon's window.'

The door goes again, and Bertie runs barking into the hall.

Brian goes to answer.

'Probably carol singers,' Mam says. 'I had a group round last night. They couldn't hold a tune in a bucket.'

When he comes back, Brian looks troubled. 'It's for you,' he says. 'It's Ginny.'

* * *

When I last saw Ginny Baker, she wore a tight red dress and expensive heels. She'd been picking her way through the debris of an almost ruined wedding, and I told myself that would be the last time we ever spoke. But even back then, a tiny voice inside suggested that matters remained unfinished.

The woman perched on of Mam's sofa in the Good Room is almost unrecognisable.

The long blonde hair has been cut short and left to grow out dark. The expensive make-up is a thing of the past.

This Ginny regards me with hollow eyes.

'I'm dying,' she says with no preamble. 'Someone told me you were down for Christmas, so I thought I'd come along and tell you firsthand. Save you hearing it from someone else.'

'My God,' I say. 'Are you all right?'

'Didn't you hear what I said? I'm dying.'

'What of?'

'Cancer. Is there anything else these days?'

She shuffles uneasily.

'Breast, metastatic into my bones. It's inoperable. They've said weeks, not months.'

'I'm so sorry.'

She nods. 'People usually are.'

Mam breaks an embarrassed silence when she pops her head round the door to offer cups of tea.

'I really caused trouble for you, didn't I?' Ginny says when we're alone again.

'It's all sorted out now. We're fine. Everything's fine.'

'And you even tried to make friends with me… that day when…'

'Yes, well, never mind. It was a strange old day, I suppose. We all said things we regret.'

'Actually, Lisa. I didn't.' Ginny gets up and walks to the window. 'I'm glad I didn't give you what you wanted.'

'OK,' I say, uncertain where any of this might be going.

'I needed to get away from here. It was what I always dreamed of doing, and honestly, you gave me the chance to disappear. Right after that wedding, I got into my car and drove. I ended up in London.'

'Someone told me that's where you were living.'

'I had a good few years there, all things considered.' Ginny stops speaking, spins around and beams at me. 'I've come here to thank you. I suppose that was your gift.'

'Thank me?'

'*I* was the one holding me back. I blamed everybody else, but it was me in charge all along. You made me see that.'

***

Ginny sips from a glass of red wine and watches everyone open presents, try on slippers and gloves, spray each other with perfume and hand around expensive chocolates.

'You did a nice thing,' Brian says as he puts an arm around me. 'Inviting her to dinner like this.'

'She's not quite the monster I used to think,' I say. 'Inside she's just the same as me.'

Bertie barks and the kids play tag. Mam sits in her armchair, enjoying the love of her family; even Glen is granted a smile despite the fluffy pink mules he insists on wearing–a gift from Amy.

***

The ambulance arrives at six thirty, just after Mam loads the dishwasher.

'You're calling her Lucinda?' Ginny says as I help her into the wheelchair. 'Loo, rhymes with Poo. That poor kid. Bullies will make her life hell. If I give you nothing else, take it from someone who knows.'

She chuckles, a raspy wheezy rattle.

As they pull away, Brian slips an arm around me.

'You OK?' he says and I nod. There's the smallest of kicks inside and I know what I have to do.

'Sophie's a lovely name, isn't it?' I say. 'Maybe we should rethink the whole Lucinda thing.'

About the Author

Born in the Midlands, and living in Brighton via Amsterdam, Mo Fanning's first book - **The Armchair Bride** - was shortlisted for the Arts Council Book of the Year in 2012. After two collections of short stories - **this is (not) america** and the festive-themed **Five Gold Rings** - and a spell writing for BBC America and The Guardian, Mo is back. **Rebuilding Alexandra Small** is due in 2021. If you'd like to know more - and get advance chapters - please sign up to Mo's mailing list.

You can connect with me on:
- http://mofanning.co.uk
- https://twitter.com/mofanning
- https://www.facebook.com/mofanningbooks

Subscribe to my newsletter:
- https://mofanning.co.uk/mailing-list

Also by Mo Fanning

The Armchair Bride
The path to true love starts with drunken new year resolutions… and the smallest of white lies.

With her fortieth birthday looming, Lisa Doyle wonders where things went wrong. Everyone from school is married with kids - or living better lives. And she should know. She's got cyberstalking down to a fine art.

Tired of feeling the odd one out, Lisa updates her online profile, adding a husband. An astronaut in training who saves lives. It's no big deal. Everyone lies online.

If only Helen could have announced her shotgun wedding sooner. And not begged Lisa to organise a hen night… for all those friends from school simply dying to meet her fabulous new husband.

Does she brazen it out, or come clean?

It sets the scene for a year in the life of an armchair bride.

www.ingramcontent.com/pod-product-compliance
Ingram Content Group UK Ltd.
Pitfield, Milton Keynes, MK11 3LW, UK
UKHW041428180426
11947UKWH00007B/345